Malcolm Jack was brought up and schooled in Hong Kong before returning to university in the UK. As a child, he learnt Cantonese at the same time as English. He has had a career both as a public servant and a writer. His writing includes articles, reviews on history, literature, philosophy, politics and a number of books. Among his travel histories are *Lisbon: City of the Sea* (2007) and *To the Fairest Cape: European Encounters in the Cape of Good Hope* (2019). His last book, *My Hong Kong* (2022), deals with writers' mainly fictional impressions of the city from the 1950s onwards. He is a frequent visitor to Hong Kong.

To family, memories, and friends.

Malcolm Jack

# MR POLLY'S BONFIRE PARTY

AUSTIN MACAULEY PUBLISHERS

LONDON * CAMBRIDGE * NEW YORK * SHARJAH

A CIP catalogue record for this title is available from the British Library.

ISBN 9781035870165 (Paperback)
ISBN 9781035870172 (ePub e-book)

www.austinmacauley.com

First Published 2025
Austin Macauley Publishers Ltd®
1 Canada Square
Canary Wharf
London
E14 5AA

A wide acquaintance with Hong Kong at every social level was my childhood experience due to the liberal attitude of my parents, Ian Ross Jack and Alicia Eça da Silva and my companion amah, Ah Lan, with whom I spoke only in Cantonese.

Many friends and acquaintances have kept my tie to the 'Fragrant Harbour' but I would particularly like to thank Cyril Wong, Kennie Ting and João Mendonça for reading the book in advance and offering useful comments.

I am particularly indebted to Gary Woollacott, whose superb proofreading has uncovered lacunae left by me in the text.

Robert Borsje has been a constant, patient listener as the plot developed.

The cover illustration deserves mention and I thank the editors at Austin Macauley Publishers for their handling of the whole project.

# Chapter 1

The gardener started his work every morning at six-thirty to avoid the scorching, midday heat. By the time Augustus John Polly returned from his early morning stroll across the campus, the gardener was reaching the flower beds in front of his house, No. 3 University Drive. His singlet was soaking wet, but Polly noticed that he still presented a neat figure; his jet-black hair neatly smoothed back. The gardener was bent forward in a crouching position, fork in one hand to cut out the weeds, a handkerchief over his head to stop sweating.

Polly came along the path just near him and blurted out in his broken Cantonese.

"A long day ahead, Ah Tang, and in this heat!"

The gardener rose from his crouching position and turned to face Polly. The early morning light emphasised the muscularity of his figure.

"Just beginning, sir, many hours ahead."

"Yes quite," said Polly, groping in his bare larder of vocabulary, "but you are doing well. Look at those neat lines."

"Not straight lines, sir," the gardener grinned. "Any boy can plant in a straight line. A man must know how to deviate."

Now it was Polly's turn to smile. Rather deep, very Oriental he thought to himself.

"Theory of Chinese gardening rests on asymmetry," he said aloud in English.

Ah Tang stared vacantly, with a good-humoured look.

"Excuse me," he managed in Cantonese as he swept by Ah Tang, who moving aside out of respect, had stepped on a plant in the herbaceous border. "You are doing a very good job."

A few minutes later, Polly was on the veranda at the front of his house. Looking down from the balcony, he could see the gardener bent over the flower bed, carefully weeding it once more. From above, Polly could see that the borders did curve slightly. Ah Tang was keeping to his asymmetrical plan. He was

9

probably the most competent person Polly would speak to today. He just got on with the job instead of making a meal of it, unlike so many of his colleagues on campus.

Ah Tang worked in a pair of tattered shorts and a holey singlet so that his smooth, hairless chest could be seen clearly in its well-formed line. Polly marvelled at the jet-black, straight hair of the figure bent over the grass, and he admired the pleasing curve that ran along from the back of the gardener's neck down his triangular-shaped torso to his compact, tight rump. Polly fancied he could smell the scent of the gardener's Oriental sweat, a smell that always reminded him of caraway seeds. Gazing with pleasure upon the young man at work, Polly began to feel something stirring in his white underpants which was all he had on in the tropical heat of the morning. Thankful for his lifelong devotion to the Egyptian cult of Amun, slowly, deliberately and with a sinful sense of luxury, he cajoled, teased and brought to a pitch his painfully stiff partner in lasciviousness. It took but a short time for that rapturous friend and collaborator to be satisfied, and once done, Polly was able to sink back into his rattan chair and glory once more at the silence of the early morning.

Rousing himself from his reverie, Polly got up from his chair and disappeared indoors. Stripping off his shorts, he clambered through the plastic curtain into the shower room and sprayed by the sprouting round, metal shower head, he luxuriated under the flow for five minutes, guilty because everyone was asked to minimise the amount of water they used during the dry season of shortages. Polly justified his behaviour by convincing himself that he needed to be sharp and alert for the day ahead. Otherwise, how could he perform properly in class? The students would be respectively silent but they would be judging his every word. Still dripping wet and wrapped in his towel, he re-emerged on the balcony, with another comforting if less sensual pleasure in his hands—his morning cup of tea. Polly preferred to make the first tea of the day himself before Ah Hing arrived to fuss and bustle in the old-fashioned, dark kitchen downstairs.

Over the years, he had cultivated a considerable connoisseurship in tea. Long gone were the dark, stewing mugs of PG Tips which had been his constant companions in his student days in England. From tea with milk, he had graduated to sweet-scented jasmine, then to refined Yunan and finally to rare Oolong given him by Clarence Lam, the brightest of his students. Polly's taste had refined, like the wine-taster's, by cultivation, so that now only the finest, most delicate flavours could satisfy his discriminating palate.

Perhaps to annoy him, perhaps from sheer ignorance, Ah Hing would never make tea in the way that he wanted. Her tea was always too strong and needed milk. Ah Hing, though in her heart against all 'foreign devils' insisted that her former master, Colonel Hicks, the district officer, had always taken milk in his tea. For her part she found that any Englishman who did not take milk in his tea was a creature to be despised or strictly, doubly despised, first for being a foreigner and secondly for not being an abominable foreigner as all foreigners should be. When Polly demanded something weaker, a watery concoction was produced, entirely devoid of taste. Ah Hing's tea invariably ended up being poured down the kitchen sink, something that offended Polly's suburban instinct against waste. There was nothing for it but to make his own cup before she arrived.

Ah Hing arrived early, disturbing Polly in his peaceful morning meditations. Rushing upstairs as soon as she had entered the house and still panting from her clamber up the deceptively steep path of the hill, Ah Hing wheezed out.

"Master, tlouble, tlouble…"

"Trouble?" Polly said, rolling his 'r'. "What kind of trouble?"

"Lioting in Wanchai, master 'big lioting, plice'. Smoke and fier. Polis car bulning."

"Rioting," said Polly, rolling his 'r' again "Police car on fire?"

"Vely selious. Levolution," said Ah Hing with a sudden gleam in her eye and then, after a pause for effect, she added, "end of capitalism."

"End of what, Ah Hing?" The usually imperturbable Polly shouted. "How on earth do you know about capitalism or for that matter any other kind of ism?"

"No, not Missens," intoned Ah Hing, whose hair Polly now noticed was newly permed. "Missens away."

Fool, thought Polly, she thinks I am referring to Meissen, the Faculty Dean and Pro Vice-Chancellor who, as everyone knows, had been given special permission to dig for terracotta warriors in a distant part of Hunan province, and who was no doubt happily doing so at this very moment.

"Thank you, Ah Hing," he said, "please make my tea and go—not too strong today," he added with a grimace. Ah Hing stood her ground for a moment. What proper master sits about in underpants? She thought to herself staring at his state of undress. She had only ever seen Colonel Hicks' under-vestments in the wash and even then they were still heavily starched. Her expression relaxed into a fawning, artificial smile and she backed away, leaving Polly no more irritated

11

than he usually was at her arrival. The fact that Ah Hing was a Communist did not particularly worry him; he had guessed that after she had come, during the fierce fighting on the mainland, tear-stained but defiant to ask for three days' leave. Her brother, a young Red Army corporal had been killed in action. No, he did not blame her. In her position, he might have been a Communist himself. It was not Ah Hing's politics that disturbed him; it was her uncompromising peasant conservatism that he could not abide.

Polly got up from his veranda chair. It was no use. His peace had been entirely shattered by Ah Hing's arrival; all the serenity of the early morning was lost. The excitement of seeing Ah Tang stripped to the waist was replaced by something else that now fully possessed him. It was the thought of the fire in Wanchai. He could imagine the flames flicking up in the air; the smell of the smoke, the panic of the crowds; the firefighters desperately hosing water into the air. His hands trembled as if he had started the blaze himself. He would have made sure it was a good one. Half measures would not do. Plenty of combustible material and a can of kerosene and what of those young men shouting for the Revolution? They were right: wasn't it about time? The smug colonial society needed shaking up.

He walked briskly into his study and started looking across the bookshelves. Brushing past the sonorous volumes of Gibbon, he ignored portentous Macaulay and next to him the weighty shelf of the historian-philosophers, Collingwood, Berlin and lurking behind them, the great German masters. Moving towards the shelf marked 'Revolution', his eye fell upon the *Little Red Book* next to the volumes of Marx. He picked it up. Here were the *pensées* of the venerable leader, Chairman Mao. Polly opened the book at random and found himself in a section dealing with the organisation of democracy. The first sentence he read was utterly commonplace and uncompromisingly dour:

*All decisions of any importance made by the Party's higher bodies must be properly transmitted to the lower bodies and the Party rank and file…*

Polly read on:

*The lower bodies of the Party and the Party rank and file must discuss the higher bodies' directives in detail in order to understand their meaning thoroughly and decide on the methods of carrying them out.*

Not much room for manoeuvre there, thought Polly. No provision for any disagreement about the decisions of the 'higher bodies'. The higher body, could, in fact, decide anything, like a policy of obliterating the lower bodies. Once these inferior organs understood the decision thoroughly, they would have to carry out their own extermination. But they wouldn't. Of course, this was a dictatorship but with half the population of China starving and the government thoroughly corrupt and in the grip of foreigners, what other solution was there? Drastic action had to be taken. Polly recalled Han Suyin, the 'Red Doctor' saying she was not a Communist, but supported the Revolution as the only way to change things for the better. She was a Chinese patriot. In the current political climate that made perfect sense. The old brigade in charge of government would never undertake significant reform. He was sure of that.

Polly paused. Suddenly he was aware of an interruption. It did not come from outside, it wasn't a machine whirring or an engine revving in the distance. Instead, the sound was a monotonous buzz, like that made by a mosquito circling round its weary victim in the middle of a sultry night. It was coming from within his head and it was getting louder. God how he hated that buzzing! How annoyed he was when the nervous, young Cantonese doctor told him that there was nothing wrong with him, suggesting, fatuously, that he might have got some water in his inner ear after his daily swim in the university pool. Polly consulted various colleagues but got no further. The most ingenious as well as idiotic explanation had come from Anthony Bridges, the senior lecturer in the philosophy department.

"Well, Polly," said Anthony Bridges, in his annoyingly superior way, "I think it's the music of the spheres you hear, the great battles in the ether. Just a bit of metaphysical ache, brought about by carrying the burden of history, nothing more than that, nothing to worry about."

At first, Polly was offended. Just another example of Bridges' Oxonian facetiousness, he thought to himself. Yet when he considered the buzzing attacks more carefully, he had to admit that they usually coincided with the point in an argument or stream of thought when he could no longer accept the logic of what he was hearing. It was as if his brain could not accommodate the sheer irrationality of what confronted it and in a strange form of protest, started to block out external reality by issuing its own noise. It was a somewhat fantastic explanation, but could it be true? The buzzing, which came without warning could sometimes last for half-an-hour at a low rumbling pitch but, at other times, it grew rapidly to a pitch of intensity that was painful. Polly had come to recognise that in this, more intense form, it did not last long, usually some two or three minutes at the most. Towards the end of the attack, the pitch of the sound changed. Gradually, the sound lessened and hardly had Polly realised it when it had ceased altogether. Occasionally, the buzzing threatened without materialising like a tooth that suggests it is about to ache and then subsides. But it was only with the return of silence and the realisation that he could once again hear his own thoughts, that Polly knew that he was quite clear of the attack. But there would be a next time.

In his study, reading Chairman Mao's *Little Red Book*, the attack lasted exactly three minutes. Polly could be precise because it had started as the clock struck the half-hour and ended when Ah Hing marched in with his soft-boiled eggs three minutes later. Considerably irritated by Ah Hing's earlier behaviour, Polly said nothing as she put down a large tray, which had on it, next to the eggs, a decent portion of toast in a silver holder, a jar of English marmalade and tea, black as ink, which he would not drink. Instead, he flicked on the radio, narrowly avoiding smearing it with the thick-cut marmalade that he had spread on the toast.

*And later this morning, His Excellency the Governor, Sir Reginald Fogerty, will meet army and police chiefs to assess what strategy to follow to contain the riots...* boomed out the silky Rediffusion voice.

Polly started up and began to pay attention.

*Although things are now calm, damage to buildings and other property in the Wanchai district is estimated to run to several million dollars. Banks have been particularly targeted. Among those arrested have been several Hong Kong University students, including Mr Clarence Lam, a second-year history student...*

Polly choked on his toast. Clarence Lam! He could not believe it. Clarence was undoubtedly his star pupil; even the overbearing Anthony Bridges who supervised his subsidiary subject, moral philosophy, had to admit that Clarence was bright. And Clarence a scion of one of the oldest Shanghai families who had come to Hong Kong at the time of the Japanese invasion of mainland China! Clever and ambitious, the Lams had got on in whatever profession they had chosen to enter. There were Lams in every important institution in the colony—

in the Hong Kong & Shanghai Bank, in the Royal Jockey Club, in the Royal Hong Kong Police. There was even a Lam, admittedly non-executive, on the Board of Jardine Matheson, the greatest of the old Taipan firms.

Good God, what would the dean do when the news reached his ears that students of his had been involved in a riot? Didn't bear thinking about it.

No sooner had Polly thought the thought when, as if in response, the black-handled telephone on the right of his rosewood desk (a reward Polly had given himself after winning the Turner Essay Competition the year before) began to tinkle.

Polly picked up the receiver gingerly.

"Pliss hold for some moment…" shrilled the operator's disembodied voice.

For a while nothing happened. Polly heard a series of clicks and some gruff exchanges in a dialect he recognised as not being Cantonese. Then there was a voice that he knew only too well: it was the dean's.

"Meissen here, Polly."

"Good heavens, Dean," said Polly, "I thought you were in Hunan." He immediately bit his tongue at his own foolishness.

"I *am* in Hunan, damn it, Polly. Telephones do work long distance you know."

"Of course, Dean. Excuse my stupidity, but I have just had a nasty shock from listening to the news."

"Oh, the Lam business, no doubt," said the dean, almost nonchalantly.

"We've been watching him for some time. All that Marxist stuff, forever thumbing the *Little Red Book.*"

Polly flinched, looking at his own copy lying on the desk. Involuntarily he reached for his lecture notes and covered the small book with them.

"Marxist-Leninist according to Bridges," the dean continued, "Polly… Polly, are you still there?"

"I'm still here," stuttered Polly, "but I had no idea about Clarence being arrested. I should have been told. No one thought to consult me," he added bitterly. "I mean after all, I am his…"

The dean cut him short.

"Now look here, Polly. Do wake up. I've told you we know all about Lam. Reported him myself, actually. Spoke directly to his uncle, Chief Inspector Chan. He didn't let the family tie stop him, a very decent sort. Not my college, but reliable Oxford man."

Polly winced. These tiresome Oxbridge people, he thought to himself, do they never give up their absurd, adolescent pretensions? Did he go about telling everyone that his erstwhile SOAS classmates now governed most of Africa and the Middle East?

"Polly, Polly?"

"Yes, Dean."

"For God's sake, wake up, Polly. Lam will be released tomorrow morning. It's just a way of shaking him up and any other fellow-travellers who might be about. The chief inspector and I agreed that that was what they needed: a bit of shock treatment. Now, what I am really calling you about is this. I won't be able to make the next faculty board and Hopkinson, who usually acts as secretary is still at Columbia talking about Ming vases. Bridges…"

The line crackled. Then the booming voice came back.

"Bridges will be in the chair and you, Polly, you will take the minutes. Polly, do you hear?"

The dean's voice was ascending on what the students called the Meissen scale of irritation.

"Loud and clear, Dean. Don't worry about the minutes. Don't give them another thought…"

There was a sudden click. Polly called out the dean's name, but there was no answer. He tapped the cradle of his phone several times until the tired voice of the university operator came on again.

"No mole line, Mr Polly. Missens gone."

Polly replaced the receiver on the hook. So, the dean had hung up on him without as much as a word of farewell. Well, that was Meissen all over; he shouldn't really be surprised.

He began to consider what the dean had said about Clarence Lam. It was not an edifying business. A student being spied upon reported to the dean without him, his tutor, even knowing; perhaps even under surveillance during tutorials in this very room, in this study at No. 3, University Drive. Now he remembered a curious incident from the previous term. One of Clarence's fellow students, one Henry Wu, had been caught, in flagrante, rifling through Clarence's personal papers. He had waited until Clarence was in a tutorial before breaking into his room. It was a nasty business. Yet when the matter had been referred to the dean, nothing had happened. Henry Wu was not charged, nor even castigated. There was no question of anything being done about it. Everyone behaved as if nothing had happened. Mr Polly had been surprised at Anthony Bridges' apparent nonchalance.

"Oh, I don't think Wu meant any harm, my dear fellow."

"So, he has done nothing wrong, Anthony?" Polly retorted. "That comes oddly from you as a moral philosopher, if I may say so."

But Anthony Bridges did not rise to the bait. He said nothing and continued to read his copy of *Mind*, buried in a battered armchair in his favourite corner of the Senior Common Room.

Now Polly knew: it had all been a stitch-up! Wu had obviously been told what to do by the dean. He was probably searching Clarence's room at the very time when Clarence was at Polly's tutorial. How naive he had been.

Polly stacked the lecture notes on his desk. Picking up the *Little Red Book*, he crossed the room and put it back on its shelf, less prominent once it sat in its row of radical, political philosophy. Then he returned to his desk and picked up the telephone again.

"Anthony, its Polly here," he muttered into the receiver.

"Ah, my dear fellow," boomed back the oleaginous Bridges. "I thought it might be you."

"Is it philosophy you teach or clairvoyance?" Mr Polly said in a tone of pretended irony, and before Anthony Bridges could respond, he continued, "Anthony, did you know about Clarence?"

There was a brief silence.

"Did I know what about Clarence?"

"Haven't you heard the news?"

"Oh, Wanchai and all that. Sorry, Polly, at first I thought you were putting an epistemological problem to me. You know the problem of other minds—how do I know if what I see—let's say it is Clarence coming to tutorials—is the same as what you see? Do we have a system of common symbols with corresponding signification? That sort of thing."

"Anthony, how much did you know before today?" Mr Polly said, determined not to be side-tracked by another of Anthony Bridges' clever evasions.

There was another silence.

"Well, if you mean did I suspect that Clarence Lam was a Communist, the answer is yes, of course, I did. I told Meissen about Lam at least a year ago. At first, the dean found it hard to believe. Said that Lam came from the top drawer, a reliable family even though Chinese. How could Clarence, the brightest of the lot, be so foolish? Well, I said to the dean, isn't that where they all come from—the bolshies, I mean, from the top drawer? Anyone who has been to Cambridge would know all about that."

Polly groaned aloud.

"It seems that everyone on the campus knew what was going on except me, Clarence's moral tutor. Why wasn't I told? What does that say about our system? What does that say about my powers of observation?"

"Oh, very little," said Anthony Bridges, with a tone of mock assurance. "I've told you many times before that I don't believe in all that scientific observation business. You'd be better off to follow your nose, I mean nous of course. Start from basics. Build upwards. Rely on logic, it's better than all that empiricism, I can assure you."

Another pause.

"By the way," continued Anthony Bridges, "Clarence always said that he first learnt about the *Little Red Book* from you. Claimed that it was on your shelf, next to Marx and Hegel."

Polly froze. He glanced over at the shelf and the books were arranged exactly as Clarence had said they were. This was becoming unpleasant. He began to wonder if his study too had been searched by the sinister Chief Inspector Chan's lackeys. They could easily have got in; nothing was ever locked up, not even the front door of the house so a raid on his study would be easy. Could they read English? Could they read German? He supposed that they could.

"But going back to your problem about historical method," continued Anthony Bridges relentlessly, "It's a question of the coherence theory of truth, old boy. You need some system, not just a paltry correspondence between observation and truth. Correspondence only leads to silly, amateur detective-novel stuff. Nothing of substance, dear fellow, nothing enduring."

Polly no longer knew what Anthony Bridges was talking about. All he did know was that he was feeling slightly giddy, and he noticed that his hand on the receiver was sweating and leaving marks on its smooth, dark surface. In the background, he began to hear a faint humming.

"Thank you, Anthony," he tried to whisper but no sound came out from his lips. Like the dean before him, he hung up without a word of farewell.

# Chapter 2

Gin and tonic, pink gin, gin and lime, Singapore sling, the dean's gin, Anthony's gin, Faculty gin, Gordon's gin: the whole spring was passing in a haze of gin. Somehow it seemed that the faculty could only function under the influence of a nightly session of alcohol served silently by sleek houseboys in the Senior Common Room. The effects of the evenings were apparent: a hush hung over the campus in the morning. Only those giving lectures or conducting seminars would be seen scurrying along the campus paths. Anthony Bridges never showed any sign of wear and tear the next morning—the sure sign of a professional drinker. He would be ensconced in his usual corner reading the daily newspapers and occasionally asking the houseboy to bring him another drink. Although the students showed no signs of knowing about these excesses, Polly realised that they must have been aware of what their teachers got up to after class. But to pretend not to know anything was so Oriental thought Polly.

He himself was feeling the effects of the latest binge as he rummaged in his chest of drawers for his black silk bow tie. He knew that he should have stopped much earlier but it had been a humid evening on the veranda, clinking glass after glass with ice from a silver bucket which Anthony Bridges had brought with him. Polly's head was thudding like a washing machine reaching the end of its spin; slow rhythmic turns made him wince with pain. It was no use. The tie had disappeared. He was sure he had put it in the top drawer of the dresser. Had Ah Hing been at it again tidying up things which she should leave alone? He tried to slam the drawer closed but it jammed. He left it hanging half open and considered what to do. There was nothing for it: he would have to go to town to get a new tie in time for the formal dinner that evening.

Carelessly dressed, in a crumpled jacket and not properly shaven he dashed along the path to the campus gates, happy not to encounter anyone. Minutes later, he was in a taxi cruising along Caine Road on his way to Whiteaway department store in Central. When he tumbled out of the taxi, he could see that the turbaned doorkeeper who swung the door open for him had a look of faint disapproval on his bearded face. "We expect our clientele to be better dressed," his expression suggested. "After all, this is Whiteaway."

Polly wandered through the Ladies' Perfumery where the colonial secretary's wife and the governor of Macao's mistress, old school chums, were spraying themselves with the latest Parisian fragrances while their single bodyguard, a young policeman smartly dressed in civvies was chatting up the trim sales assistant. They live on a different planet than mere mortals, thought Polly as he made his way past them. The thick blue carpets hushed the sound of his footsteps; an air of comfortable opulence radiated from the gleaming counters.

When he reached the tie counter, an unctuous sales assistant guided him away from the expensive silk cravats to the more modest, but still not cheap, range.

"It's quite alright," Polly heard himself saying, "fifty dollars is not too much. I will take that one."

"And will there be anything else, sir?" The assistant asked with a smirk, goading Polly into saving face by spending another hundred dollars on a pair of cufflinks that he neither wanted nor needed. In a flash, the links had been snapped into their dark crimson box and a few minutes later, the box was neatly wrapped and put on the counter by the gazelle-like assistant. With a swift movement, he put the tie and the wrapped box into a bag, handing Polly the hefty bill with a breezy smile. "Please pay for this at the cashier's counter," he said a facetious smile on his face.

Despite the cool interior of Whiteaway, Polly emerged hot and bothered into Queen's Road Central. The traffic roared past. I'll walk back, he decided. Better start making up for the lost two hundred dollars without delay! Polly began to wend his way down the crowded streets of Central, bustling and teeming with people strolling out into the early evening cool. He followed the tram lines which ran eastward, clambering up steep Shelley Street, passing the narrow lanes of stalls straggling up the hill. All the goods for sale were laid out on open trays for buyers to inspect. Everything was there from kitchen gadgets to birdcages. As the crowd moved along, the shopkeepers called out their wares, always at a bargain, they insisted. One or two shopkeepers stood on the pavement wondering what this foreign devil was doing with his heavy Whiteaway bag.

Polly turned into Hollywood Road, stopping at the window of an antique shop where a statue of a warrior guardian stared out at by-passers with a fierce glare: he had lost his long spear. The shop seemed empty but as Polly entered, he saw a toothless old man squatting in the gloomy interior with a steaming bowl of rice and congee, whose pungent smell offended Polly's Western nose. Continuing to slurp up his soup, the man called out. A slim, young lady in a smart dress emerged with a smile.

"A very old statue," she said in perfect English, pointing at the Temple Guardian, "would you like to buy him? It's a very old antique. We make a special price for you. And of course, we can deliver."

Polly felt the beady eyes of the Temple Guardian staring at him in a hostile way.

"No just looking," he muttered and turning quickly, rushed out of the shop.

He continued his hike towards the Upper Levels, now passing through a dubious area of gambling dens and houses of pleasure, occasionally interrupted by a conveniently located steam laundry. He stopped to catch his breath. His pause was taken to mean something else by a well-built peasant girl, with a reddish face and a tight-fitting *cheong sam*, who stood at the entrance to a filthy tenement stairway.

"Onlee ten dollals, mister," she whined, "ledy for evely ting you like."

God, where do they learn their lines? Polly thought. It would be a kindness if someone would bring out a bilingual phrase book for the use of these street girls.

He motioned her to go into the building, at the same time trying to hide his too-prominent Whiteaway bag and quickly calculating in his head how much cash he had on him. His heart was pounding, his mouth was dry and he began to feel a quiver in his stomach.

Inside the building, all was dim and dank. The girl walked silently ahead, up a flight of stairs and then towards a door at the end of the corridor which she pushed open, standing aside for him to pass. There was an unpleasant acrid smell of bodily fluids and a plate of unfinished cold fried food lay on a small table. It was completely dark but for a small red light in one corner. Polly felt slightly nauseous. He dreaded a sudden attack of buzzing in his head. In the penumbra, he could make out the girl slipping out of her dress. Then she lay on the bed, opening and closing her legs slowly in a provocative gesture. Her white skin was luminous.

Polly motioned her to be still. Quickly unbuttoning his trousers, he tugged himself vigorously, soon spraying his warm liquid over her pearl-white breasts. She jumped up with a scream and flounced out of the room in a display of disgust, not, however failing to snatch the ten-dollar note that Polly had placed on the small table near the door.

Polly was left alone at the scene of his crime. Slowly, he regained his breath. His heart was still pounding. He sat down at a battered dressing table which was in one corner of the room, squinting in the fogged mirror that was above it. Pulling the black bow tie from his Whiteaway bag, he began practising how to perfect a butterfly on his bare neck.

When Polly got home, he flung himself fully clothed on his bed and fell into a deep sleep. When he awoke an hour later, he had a bad headache. Realising he was running late, he rushed to take a shower, almost slipping on the stone floor. Drying himself, he dressed quickly, struggling in vain to make a perfect butterfly out of his black tie. Looking in the mirror, he could see that it was still crooked. It was too late to fiddle with it anymore. He snatched up his wallet and handkerchief and stuffing them into his pockets, rushed out of the house. It was a torrid evening. The high humidity made him sweat at once as he strolled down the path towards the university gates, trying not to rush. No sign of Ah Tang in the gardens at that hour which was more of a pity, he thought. But the gardener's work was evident: the flower beds were neat; the overhanging branches of the trees had been trimmed.

At the university gates, Clarence Lam was waiting, sleek and cool as he always appeared. His manner betrayed no sign of his night locked in a prison cell after the riots in Wanchai. Polly knew that the matter would not be mentioned by anyone including his faculty colleagues. Laura Li, dressed to the nines, stood next to him. She could have been going to a reception at Government House.

"Golly," said Clarence jovially, "you look a bit hot, Mr Polly. Sure you will be up to the snake soup we are starting the feast with?"

Polly's Anglo-Saxon stomach turned even though he knew that Clarence was joking.

"That's nonsense, Clarence," he said affably. "Chinese banquets don't begin with soup: even I know that!"

"Well done, Mr Polly," chirped up Laura Li, "don't allow yourself to be duped by the natives."

Polly smiled in acknowledgement. His eye had been caught by a prolific-flowering, blue hibiscus bush to the side of the gate and he went over to inspect it. Shrivelled, dead flowers lay strewn all over the ground around. Laura Li followed him.

"Quite a display, isn't it?" She said. "But the flowers only last one day. Tell me, Mr Polly, what brought you here to China in the first place instead of going to Turkey? After all, your precious Ottomans never got here; we managed to keep everyone out, Mr Polly, out of the motherland."

"Except the Jesuits," said Mr Polly, "didn't get rid of them for a hundred years."

Polly remembered another blue flowering hibiscus. Another torrid evening on the other side of the vast land mass facing Asia. The small, smoky bar and then the police. The hot, squalid police station. "We have a report from the Pera Palace Hotel. Two fires started in one week. Can you guess how they might have started? Who might have started them?"

Polly had tried to remain as calm as possible though a panic gripped his stomach. If he showed fear, he was done for. No use babbling about the rule of law. There wasn't any. No use demanding to see HM Consul, could take weeks. Then he knew what they wanted. He put an American fifty-dollar bill on the table. The door of the police charge room was opened for him and he stumbled with relief into the ever-bustling crowds of Taksim Square.

How vividly he could see it all again. Suddenly, the spell was broken. Forcing himself back to the present, Polly replied to Laura's question.

"I came here, to Hong Kong"—he deliberately avoided saying China which he was sure she had used to provoke him—"to meet people like you, dear Laura, and to enjoy the sight of the blue hibiscus," he added frivolously.

Laura Li made no reply. Polly felt that she was about to say something more, but held back. Once or twice before she had appeared to be about to reveal more of her private thoughts, but had stopped short of doing so. And what did she know about Polly that the others didn't? Could she have been talking to Ah Hing about the master's strange excitement when hearing about the fire in Wanchai? And why would she be spying on him in any case?

At that very moment, they were joined by Clarence Lam who seemed less at ease than he had been only minutes before. He tried to appear unruffled.

"Time to get in the taxis," he said breezily, fixing Laura Li with a stare that suggested she should leave Polly alone.

Half an hour later, they had arrived in Aberdeen. There was chaos of activity at the jetty pier. A crowd of small boats and sampans lined the side. Their owners, who did a brisk business in ferrying the gourmand diners to-and-fro to the great converted barges, jostled one another to get customers. One persistent lady screamed out, then abruptly herded Polly and the others onto her boat, balancing herself on the stern as she pushed it off the jetty. From there she steered them through the crowded water, shouting at other boat holders to move out of her way. Tough-looking men rowing other boats steered away, obeying her commands. She was obviously not a person to be crossed. Only a woman could have got away with it, thought Polly.

Ten minutes later, the group was installed on the first floor of the floating restaurant, surrounded by junks and sampans and dozens of tiny craft. The evening was pleasantly cool and a shimmer of moon shone through the clouds. Soon trays of food were being brought to their table by waiters in crisp white uniforms. The offering was exquisite and literally spectacular—whole lobsters in garlic, piquant crabs, deep-fried squid, sweet and sour garoupa, ink-like octopus in sesame, sizzling Sichuan prawns, rice cooked in three styles. They could choose which fish they wanted, which was then flipped out of the large baskets hanging on the side of the vessel, still alive. Once chosen it was passed down a row of cooks, each of whom had an allotted task in its preparation—head, tail, fins removed—before it was tossed in a deep wok and fried. Then it was brought steaming to the great round table at which they sat, with a centre that could rotate so as better to receive the pointed chopsticks that attacked the plates from all directions. Course followed course in what seemed an endless series of dishes. And the soup at the end was shark fin.

As luck would have it, Polly found himself sitting next to Fiona Meissen, the dean's wife, whose fragrant charm was such a refreshing contrast to her husband's frowsy ill-temper. How a lady of Fiona's sharp wit and winning ways could have married an old rhinoceros, like Meissen was one of Anthony Bridges' 'eternal mysteries' Polly thought to himself. With her radiant smile and relaxed manner, she was adored by the students, envied by the faculty wives and admired by all their husbands. Fiona Meissen sailed through life effortlessly with all the aplomb of someone for whom every door opens at a touch and every stairway is carpeted in red.

Polly was about to utter some light-hearted pleasantry to Fiona Meissen when Laura Li leaned across the table, determined to prevent any cosy tête-à-tête between them.

"Do tell us, Mr Polly," she said, "why it is that you reject out of hand a Marxian view of history? After all, isn't it nearer your 'ultimate history' than any liberal or Whig theory one might espouse?"

Before Polly could reply, Clarence Lam rushed in, spicing his remarks with his characteristic, gentle irony.

"As a matter of fact, I think that Mr Polly does subscribe to a Marxian view of history," said Clarence. "It's the only interpretation I can put on his comments on my last essay which pointed out the operation of the dialectic even in Ottoman court politics!"

"That's nonsense, Clarence, as you know very well. But I am not going to be drawn into an argument tonight," said Polly, "not when the shark fin soup is so delicious and the company so agreeable. It would be a foolish waste of time."

Fiona smiled approvingly at Polly.

"Quite right, dear Polly, let's leave tutorials on the campus where they belong. It's such a pleasant evening, let's talk about the food. Who can explain to me how these wonderful steam dumplings are kept so fresh?"

Laura Li bit her tongue; she knew that she had been silenced. No one dared to argue with the dean's wife.

At that moment, the dean himself turned away from Hopkinson, a lecturer in Polly's department and began speaking, *sotto voce*, to his wife. Polly took the chance to study the dean's familiar face, one that he saw day after day, in the Senior Common Room, on the campus, in the lecture hall. He had to admit that Meissen was a distinguished-looking man in a conventional way. His eyes, a fierce navy blue, were set evenly apart, lidded and slightly reptilian; his nose was aquiline, his cheeks a battered rouge colour. Most surprising of all was Meissen's mouth. It was small and delicate, his lips almost femininely curved. It was nature's joke, thought Polly to himself, to remind us, perhaps that Meissen was human after all and not just a bully. No wonder the students were frightened of him; being summoned to the dean's office was always something to be dreaded. The best thing was to keep out of his way as much as possible.

Meissen now addressed Anthony Bridges but in a voice loud enough for everyone to hear.

"Well, Anthony, you will be taking the Chair at the faculty meeting when I am away next on the conference circuit. I'm sure you'll do it well."

"With pleasure," said Anthony Bridges in an unctuous tone. He avoided looking at Polly.

So, it was settled. Once again Polly, who was considerably senior to Anthony Bridges, had been passed over, snubbed, humiliated. Always in the background; never taken seriously. Ever the Reader and never the professor. And no doubt, the dean would try to embarrass him further by asking about progress on his book, a work which had been in prospect for a decade or more.

"Polly, what's happening about your history of the Seljuk sultans?" The dean's voice came exactly as Polly had anticipated.

"It comes along, Dean."

"What, at the rate of a decade for each year you are covering?" Hopkinson spat out viciously.

"I was distracted by an article I am preparing," said Polly ignoring Hopkinson's testy intervention.

"Indeed!" said Meissen, "and what is the article about and where will we read it?"

"It's about how history has to be written," then pausing for effect, he added, "for *History.*"

Hopkinson spluttered over his noodles which he was having difficulty lifting from his bowl with his chopsticks. Just as Polly thought: the very mention of the journal was enough. Good, thought Polly. Hopkinson, a mere lecturer needed to be reminded of his place. He, Polly, was a Reader: let him not forget that. Polly the Reader and soon Polly the Writer!

"Gosh, you've been quiet about that, Polly," stuttered Hopkinson, "commissioned by them, then?"

Polly was now aware that everyone was looking at him and that he must have appeared flushed under the brilliant lighting that the Chinese insisted upon in their restaurants.

"Well," he shrugged, "not everyone is interested in 'ultimate history', so I didn't want to be a bore and broadcast it around."

There was a general gasp. So, Polly was about to publish something, perhaps something significant on the subject he had so often mentioned in his classes. Polly glowed under the stares of approbation and envy. How fickle were faculty folk, he thought, just the mention of something vaguely glamorous and international and suddenly they are all yours! Moments ago, they had dismissed him as someone who would never make the top grade. Always the Reader never the professor. Now, just because he mentioned a smart publication, their attitude changed. All to do with status, not a hoot or bother about learning for its own sake; all that stuff and nonsense that they peddled to the students. What a bunch of hypocrites.

Polly did not feel it necessary to say that not a word of his piece on 'ultimate history' had yet been written. It was enough that the idea of it was in his mind that he had thought of a sequence of logic arrived at a radical conclusion and had even assembled the opposite quotations for footnotes. No, the actual carrying into effect of the idea was a mere mechanical function. What was important was to have the creative impulse, the inspiration to understand the nature of reality. A few days of concentrated effort and it would simply pour out. Then everyone would be startled by his brilliance!

"It's as much directed at your lot, the thinkers…" he sneered in the direction of Anthony Bridges, "as to our, historical fraternity," he said patronisingly addressing the clearly agitated Hopkinson. "But another word I cannot say. The editor of the journal is punctilious you know; we contributors are not supposed to discuss articles in advance of publication."

There was a brief silence during which Polly noticed Fiona Meissen smiling sweetly at him.

"I think this calls for a toast," she said as the dean's eyebrows raised slightly.

"Shall we drink to Polly, and to 'ultimate history'?" she said crisply, raising her glass.

"To Polly and 'ultimate history'," rang out the voices from the floating restaurant.

# Chapter 3

Laura Li was Clarence Lam's great chum. They always sat together in class, looking as if they were a couple. They took it in turns to ask questions at the end of lectures as if they had synchronised everything in advance. Her questions were sharper; Clarence's more diplomatic. Impeccably dressed in the latest fashion (her family owned a fleet of merchant ships), Laura looked as if she was on her way to a society wedding rather than to a lecture, with matching shoes and handbag, sometimes a string of pearls in a long necklace above her dress line. Her face rouged, fingernails painted, Laura was a veritable *femme fatale*. Frightfully clever too, frightfully clever and what was more, diligent. When Polly suggested, as an option, that his students should attend a series of lectures in the Architecture Department, Laura Li was the first to take it up, notebook in hand. After each talk, she bombarded the newly arrived lecturer with questions, some of which he struggled to answer. She was relentless. Her behaviour was reported back to Polly.

When Polly mentioned a relevant lecture in the philosophy department, once again, Laura Li had been there. Sitting in the front row, she started taking notes and once again made her presence felt; this time to Anthony Bridges who was giving the lecture. When he had reached the end and before he could gather his papers to leave, she bombarded him with questions, demanding to know the meaning of certain words he had used. Surely there were contradictions in what he had been saying. How could they be reconciled? What a Sappho! What an Amazon! Somehow her energies had been released in a way they were not when she was squabbling over dates or obscure footnotes in *History*.

Polly remembered discussing Laura Li's prowess with Anthony Bridges after the occasion when she had regaled him with impossible questions. It had been an insufferably hot summer afternoon at the end of her first year. Both dons had been sitting in the philosopher's deliberately darkened room, the blinds drawn down to keep out the afternoon glare, the ceiling fan whirring furiously without any effect that they could feel. Outside the sun was beating relentlessly down on the campus pathways. They were reclining in Anthony Bridges' capacious armchairs, each clutching a huge pink gin, even though it was only four o'clock in the afternoon. Anthony Bridges, normally sleek and unruffled, was red-faced and breathless; the line of sweat on the back of his shirt made him stick to the leather chairs when he tried to get up to refill the glasses.

"Oh, devil of a girl. She turned up again the other day. We had the most awful row in class. You know how devoted Susan Chowder is to her Bayle and that wretched *Dictionary* of his—should damn well be called an encyclopaedia anyway."

Polly thought of the drab Susan, with her freckled face and in her tired summer frock, famous among the students for being able to distinguish which Chinese toadstools could be eaten safely and which were deadly poisonous. In his mind's eye, he contrasted her messy, student-like appearance with that of the immaculate Laura Li. Susan Chowder seemed to the students to be the archetypical absent-minded academic. Obviously learned, she seemed incapable of sticking to a clear theme making her lectures difficult to follow for freshers. However, no one complained: it just wasn't in the Oriental character to cause embarrassment for the teacher.

"Well," continued Anthony Bridges, "Laura turned up with a whole raft of those famous cross-references of Bayle, you know, the beastly *renvois*. She insisted that he had got it all wrong. Had gone up the proverbial gum-tree. A worse mess than Descartes ever got himself into with the mind/body morass. Well, as you can imagine, Susan went through the roof."

She turned a bright puce colour, only just managing to spit out words in defence of her hero. There was an embarrassed silence in the lecture room; the atmosphere was tense.

Laura Li said nothing. Instead, she smiled her triangular face aglow with satisfaction at having roused Susan's anger.

Then she spoke with quiet confidence.

"If only it were so, Dr Chowder,"—the title was used with deliberate irony— "but look at these two references I have for you on accident and substance. Entirely contradictory. Here he says that accident is a self-sufficient entity, while there he says, agreeing with the church fathers, that accident has no independent existence."

"But Missss Leeee; it's the contradicdicdic-tion that BBBBayle is exposing…" came the sharp retort. Her stammer became worse when she got excited.

"Ah," beamed Laura, moving in for the kill, "but look what he says about the conditions that must attach if one proposition contradicts another. They don't fit this case. So he is in a muddle, one way or the other."

There was an audible gasp in the lecture room; everyone was aghast and unsure of what would happen next. But this time Laura did not wait, getting up quickly and snatching her bag and notebook, she swept out of the room with an air of a successful marksman who had got his kill. There was a stunned silence in the lecture room. No one uttered a sound. Susan Chowder resumed her lecture, but her stutter had not subsided.

"Golly, sounds as if I got off quite lightly then," said Polly. "All we argued about in my class was the significance, in the context of court politics, of a shift in the residence of the Grand Vizier in 1654."

"Hardly a matter of the eternal verities, old boy. But do have a top-up of your glass," urged Anthony Bridges who was beginning to feel restored by the vast quantity of gin he had consumed.

"Do you think there is anything bothering her, Laura I mean?" Polly asked noticing that Anthony Bridges hesitated before speaking.

"What do you mean, Polly?"

"Well, I just wonder if there is something underneath all these outbursts. Some form of protest?"

Anthony Bridges did not answer. His expression suggested that he did know something about Laura, but was not willing to share it with Polly. Instead, he changed the subject asking Polly what he intended to do during the half-term break.

By the time Polly left Anthony Bridges' study, the sky had darkened ominously. A typhoon was on the way and soon the storm signals would be raised. First No. 1 when there was still uncertainty about its route, then No. 3 as its course was more certain and from number 3, a straight leap to number 9 which meant that Typhoon Lisa was on a direct line for the colony. Schools and government offices closed, followed by banks and department stores. The streets were filled with office workers streaming out of buildings, clutching briefcases and bags filled with confidential documents. Soon even the jewellery shops and restaurants, whose owners hated to lose business, had to follow suit. Shutters came down. Last of all were the brothels whose doors never closed at any time of year. After all, it was only mid-afternoon: the day's business lay ahead.

The students and staff at the university had all been sent home. Dean Meissen was in his element. First ordering everyone to leave, he then issued instructions to everyone living on campus: on no account were they to go out of their houses or flats. Anyone disobeying these instructions would be punished. The old military man hidden in him had suddenly returned. Everything was strangely calm. Polly found it eerie, in the middle of the afternoon, to walk along a completely deserted university path and gaze at the empty lawns, abandoned even by the assiduous Ah Tang, the gardener. The air was still and oppressive. Even the insects, the cicadas, frogs and buzzing bees had fallen silent. The only sound to be heard was the hollow hooting of an owl, tricked into thinking that it was night by the heavy, overcast sky.

When the storm came, it came with a fury, tearing up trees, moving cars and whipping up huge waves around the harbour. Part of the sea defences collapsed, adding debris to the wild, swirling waters. Ships were lashed off their moorings and flung against piers, buildings swayed dangerously and roofs were ripped off with mad abandon as if nature were wreaking revenge on mankind. The frail wood and tin huts of the squatters on the hill above the ironically named 'Happy Valley' were tossed into the air. The miserable dwellings that were nevertheless home were flattened with a few furious blasts. Then came torrential rain pouring down the mountainside and flooding the streets below. Soon nullahs were overflowing. Mud came down from the slopes burying makeshift street stalls.

Polly felt restless. Sitting at his desk, he could hear the wind whirling around the house, trying to force its way through the battened-down shutters. He kept getting up to check the barometer which indicated severe storms would continue. Impatiently, he picked up the phone and dialled the number for University Hall. Typhoon or not, he did not fancy making do with Ah Hing's greasy leftovers, stuffed in the fridge, for dinner.

The phone rang for what seemed an interminable length. At last, it was answered.

"Solly, Mister Polly, no dinner tonight, no one come, big winds. You not go out in Dai Fung; Missen say all stay inside."

Polly slammed the receiver down so that the phone shook in its cradle. He was annoyed. Meissen again was trying to control everyone's life as if they were all silly children. But he, Polly, was not going to be kept in by that bully. He picked up the receiver again and dialled. In a few moments, the unctuous, smooth voice of Anthony Bridges came over the line.

"Oh, dear Polly," he said in his most patronising voice, "do come and have supper with me if you can stand up against the wind. The whole place is creaking. I hope you can put up with some simple poached salmon; we can always wash it down with something decent. I've got some hock from a friend who is living in Baden-Baden. Just the right thing for the main course. And then something stronger to round things off."

"Sounds marvellous," said Polly. "Shall I come over about eight?"

The line crackled, but Anthony Bridges' voice was still audible.

"Yes, that's fine. By the way, have you found your specs yet? Wouldn't want you to be banging on the Meissen's door instead of mine in the storm. Will look like you are deliberately defying his ban on going out. We'd both be put in his bad books!" he added, with a chortle.

"Of course, I've got them," said Polly, "how do you think I managed to call you?"

"By intuition," said Anthony Bridges with his superior chuckle, a sound Polly now associated with all linguistic philosophers.

"I went back to the swimming pool and the attendant had kept them aside."

"Excellent," said Anthony Bridges, "see you at eight."

The tone went blank. Polly put back the receiver, this time gently.

Polly reflected on the recovery of his spectacles which he had lost when he went for a lunchtime swim the day before. He had arrived at precisely one o'clock at the sports centre as he usually did knowing it would be deserted at that hour. That spared him from being seen by anyone since he was proud neither of his physique nor prowess at swimming. He thought he had followed his usual routine of taking off his watch and putting it in his shirt pocket, then taking off his socks and stuffing them into his sandals, then balancing his spectacles on the brim of his shoes before getting changed into his swimming trunks. But he had not. The spectacles lay on the bench nearby. What had distracted Polly was the presence of two slim, feline male students whom he recognised from the Medical School. They were changing silently when he entered, neatly piling their clothes as they put them into adjacent lockers. Seeing Polly, they started to giggle. How that giggling annoyed him! Normally, a harmless cover-up for embarrassment among the Chinese, but this time it seemed to be aimed at him, dangling and skinny in his nakedness. And why did they have to come down his row anyway, right past him? It was not the obvious route to get out of the changing room. As the boys slipped by, androgynous and sweet-smelling, Polly deliberately turned his back on them.

Soon Polly was in the pool, relaxing into a serene back-stroke, enjoying the sensation of gliding through the water, turning over at the end of the lane so that he could peer down at the light-blue bottom, with its gradual undulating shape. The two students were swimming on the far side at top speed, obviously showing off. Polly ignored them. As he glided to-and-fro, he was not thinking of anything in particular. He had trained himself to enjoy the solitariness that comes with swimming. His mind had switched itself off while he sailed up and down the lengths of the pool. If his peace was interrupted by something that was nagging him—a lecture unprepared, a meeting with the dean—Polly would allow it to last no more than the length he was swimming. Once he reached the end and was ready to turn, giving himself a gentle push from the wall with his leg, the subject had to be dropped. The ploy always worked.

Polly completed his habitual twenty lengths, allowing himself to float for a few minutes of relaxation at the end. Then he hauled himself out of the water, dismissing after an instant's thought, the idea that he might have miscounted and had actually only swum eighteen lengths. What difference did it make anyway? He thought, rebelling against his own sternness. How absurd to impose such rigidities on oneself! When he reached the changing room, he was relieved to find that it was empty. The boys had disappeared. Polly had his shower and before long was dressed again and made his way home for lunch. The spectacles remained on the bench where he had placed them.

It was half an hour later before Polly realised that he didn't have them. From the swimming pool, he had wandered into the students' canteen with its Formica table tops and polka-dot paper serviettes and, sitting in a far corner on his own, had gobbled down a dish of carbohydrates and fat. From there, he made his way back to No. 3, University Drive, seeing the fleeting figure of Hopkinson, be-gowned, on the other side of the green. As soon as he sat down at his desk in the dark, sombre study, in a flash he remembered putting them down on the bench. Rising from his desk, he left the house quickly and made his way back to the swimming pool.

The attendant's stand was empty, so he pressed the round bell on the counter. From behind a half-drawn curtain, he heard a shuffling sound. When the attendant emerged, he showed no sign of being surprised to find a dishevelled member of staff in front of him. These 'gweilos' were the strangest people, always demanding something to be done—too much chlorine in the pool; lack of towels. Their demands were never-ending.

"Ah, you have come back for these, sir," he said with a respectful nod, producing the glasses from below the wooden counter.

Polly noticed that his English was faultless, without the usual sing-song, local ring to it.

"Thank you so much, Mr," he paused.

"Hang," said the attendant, stooping slightly as he spoke, "please call me Hang, sir."

"Thank you, Mr Hang," said Polly, deliberately adding the title. He was about to turn to leave when he stopped himself and said impulsively. "How did you learn to speak English so well, Mr Hang, if you don't mind my asking?"

Hang smiled, revealing some gaps in his teeth. "Thank you, sir, as a matter of fact, I learnt English at Sandhurst, sir, Sandhurst in Surrey," he said with a grin.

Polly was surprised but tried not to show it. "So, you were trained for the British army?"

"No," said Hang enjoying the mystery he was creating. "Actually, I was in the Nationalist Army, under Commander Chiang Kai Shek. I was a colonel," he said stiffly. "Most of us were trained in England."

There was a silence. Polly stuttered slightly when he spoke.

"How difficult it must have been for you. I mean to lose such a position and then…" He broke off.

"To be reduced to being a swimming pool attendant?" Hang said in a self-mocking tone. "No, not really. We Chinese look at things differently. Sandhurst trained or not," he added, laconically.

"What do you mean?" Polly asked.

"Well, we think that the difficult thing to deal with is success. Being a humble swimming pool attendant, instead of an army colonel, is very easy. I don't have to think about discipline, about the unit, about how we are doing, about the C-in-C and all the rest of it. When I was a soldier, all that weighed heavily on me each day. I had great responsibilities. Life was difficult. I knew that if I stumbled, I would fall a long way now."

He broke off with a gentle smile. Polly stared at Hang's battered face. There was an intelligent look in his eyes. He was about to ask him how long ago he had fled to Hong Kong. But perhaps it was too personal? Instead, picking up his glasses, he muttered his thanks and left.

A few hours later, sunk in the deep recesses of Anthony Bridges' chair, holding another large drink in his hands, Polly thought of his encounter with Hang; the wizened face, the bony hands that had handed him back the spectacles. In the background, the changing rooms with their rows of slatted benches, the smell of chlorine. He could hear Hang's gentle voice, but his words floated in the air like light feathers or frail, wispy insects. Polly thought of their meaning and he felt within himself a strange sensation of lightness, a kind of weightlessness. Closing his eyes tight, he saw an image of himself floating down university path, a few feet above the ground, with his gown flowing behind him. There was a light morning mist all about him.

# Chapter 4

At first, Polly could not understand Anthony Bridges' keenness to go to the races at Happy Valley. Of course, when he thought more about it became clearer: it wasn't the horses that interested him, rather the Race Course Club was a gathering place for the great and the good. The same gathering would assemble at Government House parties or at the Pryce-Jones's. Complimentary drinks flowed from the bar. The Club was supported by the great taipan firms such as Jardine Matheson and the banks, principally Hong Kong & Shanghai. But most generous of all were the individual sponsors: rich Chinese businessmen addicted to gambling and among whom, no doubt, were plenty of Clarence's Lam relatives. And in the middle of it all was the governor's box where His Excellency might be found or other top-ranking officials.

Polly pondered on that addiction to gambling which seemed so prevalent among the local community at all levels. He knew of cases of university employees, some at quite humble stations, who had amassed serious debts. One, who earned a pittance, had raised debts of thousands of dollars. It was well above his ability to pay it back.

"It's a genetic thing," boomed Meissen, "as far as I can see an addiction in the whole yellow race." Polly winced at the dean's way of describing the Chinese but there seemed no other explanation for this particular vice. "Undoubtedly," continued Meissen, "the future of Macao will be secure because the Portuguese have allowed gambling to flourish there, unlike us with our puritanical restrictions. They handled things very cleverly and discreetly with Beijing. There is a constant stream of avid gamblers coming in from the mainland, some high up in the official hierarchy and they are not going to be stopped."

Well, at least there was something to watch when the horses tore around the racecourse, Polly thought, as he prepared for the excursion with Anthony Bridges who would be at his door at any moment. On the other hand, he could not help thinking about the squatter huts on the surrounding hills. How could such deprivation co-exist with the opulence of the racecourse attendants?

"I've ordered a cab," Anthony Bridges boomed over the phone. "Be ready in about fifteen minutes and meet me at the gates, old boy." Polly reluctantly tugged on his tie and put on a jacket in the sweltering afternoon heat. But he knew that they would not be admitted to the special box unless they were formally attired. Etiquette demanded it.

Soon the two dons were sailing along the streets of Central on their way to Happy Valley. What a misnomer, thought Polly, with the squatter camps on the hillside above the racetrack while the spoilt punters were cavorting below.

"By the way," said Anthony Bridges, "the Lams are throwing a party this time so it's going to be great fun. You know how keen they are to support their *alma mater* so we will be well looked after."

Polly nodded, wondering who else would be there. The Lams would have left nothing to chance; it would all be arranged even if people greeted one another with feigned surprise. That was Hong Kong. Half an hour later when they entered the terraced interior, there were a bevy of waiters clad in white jackets and wearing gloves serving drinks to a throng of guests already gathered. One or two pundits were at the front with binoculars trained on the track. Just as he was beginning to tire, Polly was accosted by one of the Lams—Pauline, a successful journalist. She was dressed to the nines in a summer outfit that included a wide-brimmed hat worthy of Ascot.

"Mr Polly," she said, "I did not expect to see you here. I had no idea that you were a racing enthusiast."

Polly grinned. "I could say the same thing about you, Pauline. No special assignments to keep you at the press?"

Pauline smiled and pointed to a quiet corner where they could chat together, away from the babbling crowd.

"Do you think one day," she said sipping her cocktail, "all this fun," she swept her hand at the party revellers, "will come to a standstill by a sudden interruption? Something that brings it all to a halt?"

Polly was taken aback. "You mean the squatters up there on the hillside will come swooping down?"

"Could be," she said, "or rather a more serious contingent of helmeted soldiers from you know where."

So, they were onto that subject thought Polly, he had better be careful. Especially bearing in mind Pauline's wide circle of contacts. Was it a probe? Had she been put up to it?

"Oh undoubtedly, one day it could all come to an end," he said, swirling the last of his champagne, "I think I would rather not be around to see it."

Pauline remained silent for a few moments. "Unless of course, you had wanted it to happen," she said quietly so that no one else could hear.

Polly did not reply. It was a set up; that was quite clear.

Suddenly, his thoughts were interrupted.

"I say, old chap," said Anthony Bridges, clutching another glass of champagne, "isn't this a marvellous party. I told you the Lams never do anything by halves. I just spoke to yet another of Clarence's uncles. He has an antique shop in Hollywood Road which he assures me is full of ancient, priceless pieces which I should go and view."

"Don't they all say that?" Polly said. "Remember that recent scandal involving the certification of Ming vases by one of those shops which turned out to be fakes? They had been made in Kowloon!"

"Well, *caveat emptor,*" said Anthony Bridges lowering his voice in case he was overheard by anyone in the throng of guests. "Anyhow, it's really impossible to tell the difference when they are so beautifully made. One astute collector I know mixes up priceless objects with ordinary pieces so that any burglar breaking into his house has to be quite discerning to steal the right objects."

At that moment, Pauline emerged from the back of the box and joined the two outsiders in the group.

"Gosh, super hat, Pauline," boomed Anthony Bridges, "don't you agree about the forging of Chinese antiques?"

"Certainly," Pauline replied, "you need a great deal of expertise to tell fakes from the real thing. Recently someone I know bought what was supposed to be a pair of Tang horses. By the time the forgery was discovered, the dealer who sold them had disappeared."

Their conversation was interrupted by loud clapping. In the last race of the day, the Lam horse had flashed past the finishing post ahead of the others. The jockey was doing the traditional canter around the paddock for his triumphant accolade. The enthusiasts at the front of the cocktail room cheered wildly.

"Perhaps it's time to leave," said Polly, "down that bubbly and let's go."

For once, Anthony Bridges did not demur. The smart waiters in their white uniforms had disappeared and were replaced by a bevy of Lam *amahs* clearing up the glasses. The party was over.

# Chapter 5

It was a glorious morning. The storm clouds had disappeared and there was coolness in the autumn air. Polly was in high spirits thinking that Ah Hing had the day off, so he had not been interrupted in his matinal reveries. There was nothing to do except to contemplate the delights of Clarence Lam's launch picnic. A balmy, fragrant air wafted across the balcony. There was a slight dew on the grass, everything looked fresh and inviting. Bounding from the balcony into his room, he showered, dressed and then ran along University Drive in the highest spirits. At the bus stop, he met Jennifer Sung, an introverted postgraduate student accompanied by colleague Hopkinson.

Hopkinson was full of beans and babbled on during the whole twenty-minute bus ride, while Jennifer Sung was suffering from the neuroses of postgraduate students, especially when they have taken a day off work. She sat silently, peering myopically out of the window as the morning light bathed the Upper Levels district in a golden glow. Before long the bus was plunging down the precipitous Garden Road. Ladies in white hats and gloves were sauntering out of St Joseph's Church from morning mass. Fortified by heartfelt confessions, they were able to resist with greater firmness the hawkers hovering outside the church trying to catch their attention.

At Queen's Pier, there was no sign of a launch or any of the Lams. Instead, there was the usual crowd of beggars that hung about there, living, as it appeared, on the steps of the pier that led down to the water's edge. A thin, dirty, old woman, dragging a bundle of rags, approached Polly, trying to fix him with a stare. Polly averted his gaze, but it was no use. He tried to ignore her, but the old dame would not be put off. She cringed nearby and whined until he turned around to face her. It was not an edifying sight. Her eyes seemed red and swollen, her cheeks were hollow and a few strands of grey hair hung over her forehead. When she opened her mouth to speak, she exposed a row of decayed teeth.

"*Bai gnor sup mun,*" she wailed, "give me ten dollars," pointing to her smelly bundle of old rags with a look of despair, which if feigned, was nevertheless well-acted. Polly felt uncomfortable while Jennifer Sung, emerging from her depressive silence, tried to shoo the old crone away. He took out a crumpled one-dollar bill from his pocket and as he handed it to her, he heard a voice call out.

"Now, Mr Polly, that is a gesture of conscience, but it doesn't do the slightest good. Neither that lady herself nor society benefits from random charity," said Clarence Lam, who had just arrived at the pier in an immaculate blazer, cravat, and white flannel trousers.

"Anyway, she may have stacks of those dollar bills. One of the ladies who hang about here is collected by car each evening."

"That may be so," said Polly in a tone which he knew was too sharp. "But it isn't for us to judge. We must follow our instinct in matters of this sort."

Clarence's superciliousness, in the presence of the old beggar who had backed away, annoyed him.

Clarence grinned good-humouredly.

"But isn't it the policy of the government not to give hand-outs on the grounds that the natives must be taught to fend for themselves? How can we natives do that if individuals like you go around dispensing charity whenever you feel moved to do so?"

Polly did not have time to answer for, at that very moment, a gleaming thirty-foot launch buffeted the jetty.

"Come aboard, Polly," shouted Dean Meissen in a jocular tone. He had already boarded before the launch and had been around to the pier where the others were waiting.

"Come aboard, Polly, come on, Hopkinson, Jennifer, we've got to get going. Falling behind schedule."

What schedule was there to fall behind? Polly thought, hopping on as best he could as the launch swayed at the pier and one of the crew, in sailor's uniform, tried to keep it steady with a long pole. As he scrambled aboard, a crew member held his arm to steady him. Polly took a few hesitant steps along the deck to reassure himself; his sense of balance was easily upset. He noticed that Hopkinson, with his public schoolboy assurance, had jumped on board without the slightest hesitation.

Everything was gleaming and shipshape on deck. The planks had been scrubbed, the railings were polished and the brass fittings shone. Polly was led to the stern of the ship by an immaculate seaman, whose crisp, starched whites he could not help admiring. Soon they were jugging along the shoreline past Central with its skyscrapers and through the channel at Stonecutters Island. The sun shone on the deck; the sea was a glorious green; the air salty and refreshing.

"Ah, Polly," boomed out Meissen in a friendlier tone than usual, "welcome aboard, Buck's Fizz is being served starboard."

Polly admired the way the dean used nautical terms as if they were everyday expressions for him; surely he was an army man, not a sailor?

"Come and meet Ernest Yap from the Immigration Department and Chief Inspector Chan, Clarence's uncle, our host. A most civilised character, you'll like him."

Polly tried to smile genially, but he felt something stirring in the pit of his stomach that made him uncomfortable. How embarrassing it would be to become ill the moment he had stepped aboard. He must control himself, calm down, and let the wind pass out quietly. He struggled along the narrow strip of deck between the cabin wall and the railing, anxious not to lose his balance and fall headlong into the harbour. Once at the rear, on the wider deck, where the movement was not so violent, he felt better.

A crowd was already assembled there and it was beginning to get hot. While the dean moved off in the direction of the drinks, served by two waiters in smart, white tunics, Polly looked round to see Fiona Meissen, pretty and summery in a flowery frock, Laura Li, a little plump in her short, polka-dot skirt and Chief Inspector Chan, very off-duty in a short-sleeve silk shirt and khaki trousers. Everyone was already clutching a cocktail. And there was Alistair Crowley, a fastidious bachelor from the Colonial Secretariat who had once given a lecture on ethics in the public service to the law faculty—a day before the governor sacked half of the immigration department for suspected corruption. Next to him was the inscrutable Ernest Yap, one of the few senior officers of that department who had survived the purge. Polly tried to steer himself through the group without engaging in conversation, but before he had reached the table where drinks were being served, he was waylaid by Clarence.

"Now, Mr Polly, no hiding. Do take a glass and follow me and let me introduce you to some people. Do you know Herbert and Isadora Macpherson?"

Polly picked up a chilled glass and then turned round.

"Pleased to meet you," he mumbled, remembering that Macpherson was the Director of Civil Aviation and that his daughter was studying chemistry at the university. Fair-haired and blue-eyed, she had not been easy to miss among the rows of sleek, black hair and oval faces.

"And how is…um?"

"Cathryn," said Mrs Macpherson, a buxom Scottish lady of reassuring friendliness, "Cathryn is doing very well," she continued, gurgling with parental pride, "in fact, I gather (her 'Caathryn' was a wide, Caledonian one) she may be in line for a first. Isn't that so, Dean?" She said as Meissen, clutching another full glass, joined the group. The dean smiled with an air of experienced evasiveness.

"Can never tell with scientists," he said, affecting a feigned jollity, "never quite know what's going on in that faculty," he said glaring at Polly as if it was his fault that such an awkward question had been asked.

"Unlike we happy travellers in history," interjected Clarence who realised that Polly needed rescuing.

"Now, Mr Polly, come and meet Uncle Eddie. He is longing to meet you. He is a Balliol historian, do be warned!"

Polly moved forward. He noticed that Meissen was now talking to Henry Lam from the Hong Kong & Shanghai Bank. The dean's tone was subdued, Henry Lam's sombre. Everyone knew that the university's finances were in a bad way. Perhaps he should linger and listen. No perhaps not, Meissen had his back to him, anyway. Instead, he followed Clarence who was waiting to introduce him to the chief inspector.

Eddie Chan seemed extraordinarily relaxed and affable for a senior police officer. He had a short, slightly portly figure, his thinning strands of hair combed straight across his head, rosy cheeks and a gleaming, full-toothed smile that gave him the air of a successful restaurateur, which, for all Polly knew, he might have been as well as a police inspector. Such things would not be surprising in Hong Kong. Nevertheless, thinking of what had happened at the Wanchai riots, when this jovial man must have done a deal with the university authorities or at least with the dean, Polly reminded himself to be on his guard.

"Pleased to meet you," he said, glad to extricate his hand from the chief inspector's iron grip.

"Oh, it is my privilege," said Eddie Lam, "Clarence has told me so much about you. I believe you have fascinating theories about history and the role that historians themselves play in it."

Polly smiled. "I'm sure you know that Clarence has a fertile imagination, Chief Inspector. He is a master of storytelling."

"As opposed to history?" Eddie Chan said. There was the slightest trace of irony in his impeccable English tones.

"Ah, he did warn me," said Polly, "that you yourself are an historian. No doubt, you have your own view about what an historian is doing when he writes history."

"Well, I might do," grinned Eddie Chan, "but I'd rather hear your opinion. Clarence tells me that you talk about 'objective history'—now that has a splendid Actonian ring about it, if I may say so."

Polly was amused. So, Clarence had been setting up his guests. Just spreading a little tittle-tattle too, throwing out bait for others to nibble. Oh, well, if there was to be sport, he may as well join in.

"Well, I don't claim a defence of the kind that might stand up in court," he said, with deliberate provocation, "but I think I can make out a decent case for the lecture room."

Eddie Chan waited, with the experienced dilatoriness of a wily prosecutor who knows that a witness will soon discredit his own case by saying too much.

"Of course, I know history is a selective process," said Polly, duly ruffled by the chief inspector's silence.

"Judgements enter into the historian's task at every level."

"Quite," said Eddie Chan, "even in deciding what the facts are."

"Oh, indeed," Polly continued, now throwing caution to the wind.

"The Battle of Hastings is a historical fact because we historians say that it is. There are any number of other battles of the time which are not recorded or even if they are, are deemed to be of no significance. Incidents they may be, but not part of our story."

"Not part of history," said Eddie Chan, "rather like the stealing of the gates of Kam Tin village by a nineteenth-century governor here."

At the mention of a governor, Alistair Crowley, who had his back to Clarence and the chief inspector, twitched and moved his head to the side so that he could hear what was being said. An example of political antennae, thought Polly, or perhaps just plain eavesdropping.

"I don't know about that story," he said blandly.

"Well," said Eddie Chan, brimming with amusement. "The governor of the time, one of the Pope-Hennessy tribe, fell in love with the splendid village gates of Kam Tin in the New Territories. The gates were highly ornamented and much loved by the villagers, as well. But it appeared that no one actually owned them; there was no legal document registering ownership. However, the governor was the governor, so he simply had them removed and shipped back to his estate in Ireland where he decided they would make a grand entrance to his grounds."

"Good Heavens," exclaimed Polly, "so they woke up one morning and the gates were gone?"

"Quite so," said the chief inspector, rolling his 'o' in a manner no longer fashionable even in the ancient quads of his old college.

"The irate villagers petitioned Queen Victoria. After a long delay, they received a reply: the Queen had decided, in her wisdom, that the gates, which had now stood on the boggy ground of County Meath, should be returned to Kam Tin."

"And were they?" Polly asked.

"Oh yes, of course," said Eddie Chan, "actually in a better state when they had left because, to survive the Hibernian mists, the governor had spent a lot of money having them cleaned and restored."

"So, your question is," said Polly, "is this incident just one of those forgotten things that happened, not part of history, certainly not official history or is it part of history, another history, the story of the anti-colonial struggle?" Alistair Crowley had now turned and was facing them.

"I say, Polly, what on earth you are talking about on such a wonderful, sunny morning?" He rasped, in a tone which Polly imagined him to use when he wanted to silence junior clerks in his office.

"We are only discussing the philosophical nature of history," interrupted Eddie Chan, "and I am anxious to hear Mr Polly, a distinguished historian, explain to me why it is that some facts are part of history, while others are not."

Alistair Crowley was snookered and he didn't like it. The deputy assistant colonial secretary, like the dean, was not a man to be crossed with impunity. There were stories about his revenge, always cool and well-thought out. On the other hand, Polly knew that he was one of that vast throng of pragmatic British diplomats who, strong with the weak, immediately recognised when they had to be weak with the strong. And the Lams, by God, were strong. Not only was he acutely aware of being a guest on one of the Lam launches, but he knew that their tentacles stretched everywhere. Lam brains, Lam bravado, Lam money. For all he knew, it was Lam Bay that they were even now approaching in a remote cove of Lamma Island. He swallowed his anger and waited to hear what the absurd Polly would say next. How could any man, wearing sandals and red socks at a smart Hong Kong launch picnic be taken seriously by anyone? Without being conscious of what he was doing, Alistair Crowley adjusted his spotted, silk cravat.

"Just because we have to exercise judgement about the inclusion of facts in history, does not mean that history is in no way objective," said Polly concisely. He was worried about the volume of his own voice—had he boomed out the last few words or had it just seemed that he had?

"Even a scientist must exercise some discretion about facts," he said, trying to lower his voice.

Eddie Chan showed no sign of being deafened if indeed he was.

"Yes, I understand that, Mr Polly," he said, "but how do you arrive at the universal laws that make up your 'ultimate history'?"

Polly ignored the amused grin of Clarence who had now re-joined them.

"They are induced from the facts," said Polly, "those facts properly established as historically meaningful, of course. Without the basis of valid facts, the thing just doesn't work, like a house without foundations."

Polly took a deep breath. Was it the slow, turning movement of the launch as it heaved into the bay that was making him queasy, was it the Buck's Fizz on an empty stomach, or just the headiness and passion of the words that vibrated in his head? Whatever the cause, Polly could feel his heart pounding and his hands trembling in an uncontrollable manner, as if he wanted to scale the entire keyboard of a piano in one sweep.

For a moment, there seemed to be a complete silence except for the sound of the breaking of the waves on the launch's bow. Polly's last remark, which had indeed been said in a louder than conversational tone, had brought silence to the group on deck. As one or two people stared at him—he was aware of the kindly look of concern in Fiona Meissen's eyes—Polly began to hear the familiar, still distant buzzing in his ears. He gazed out across the calm, green sea; he could see the land getting nearer. All the time the buzz increased. Before long it was very loud indeed, like an aircraft landing in a quiet, country field.

"And then you will have 'ultimate history', I mean when all issues are settled and the knowable is known," he bellowed out at the top of his voice. "All that is knowable will be known," he shouted again to reinforce the point.

Dean Meissen was the first to recover from the shock that gripped everyone on deck. He moved forward towards Polly, signalling to Clarence to help him.

"Polly, why don't you go and lie down? Go on, Clarence will take you down to rest for a short while."

Then turning to the others, he said, with authority, "It's a touch of sunstroke, nothing serious. Seen it in Malaya when a chap had too much sun in the late morning, before tiffin. Needs to lie down in the cool."

The company gradually unfroze and conversations were taken up again. But as Clarence moved towards Polly, the buzzing had reached an unbearable pitch. He screamed out maniacally.

"Even though, the predictions remain conditional, predictions that must provide necessary and sufficient conditions."

Polly was panting now, out of breath and with his lips parching and cracked. He was aware that he had gesticulated and swung his arms in the air for everyone had backed away from him. Dean Meissen carried on talking as if nothing had happened while Clarence moved decisively forward, and taking Polly by the arm, guided him into the black depths of the cabin.

# Chapter 6

When Polly woke up, he felt completely parched. There was a whirring noise not far from his head which he became aware was a small fan rotating the hot air around the cabin, and not in his head. It was still hot and the light streaming in through the porthole hurt his eyes. He could hear the tapping of shoes on the wooden deck above as people moved about. He could even hear the faint sound of conversation, not specific words, but a low, warm, human buzz. Occasionally, there was a gentle splash of water against the side of the boat. Polly realised that the engines of the launch had been switched off—they must be anchored in the bay—and one or two of the heartier guests had dived into the water. He couldn't recollect clearly what had happened on deck except that he had created a stir. He remembered Fiona Meissen looking very concerned.

Clarence suddenly appeared with a tray, on which stood a small teapot, decorated with a gaudy purple rose and two matching Chinese cups with lids. The crockery rattled as the boat swayed. Clarence stopped to regain his balance, and then carefully lowered the tray onto the flat table in front of Polly. He was naked from the waist up. His smooth, brown hairless torso gleamed in the light falling on him from the porthole. Polly admired his jet-black nipples. Pouring the tea carefully, Clarence swung himself into a small chair that was crammed in the corner of the cabin and began to sip from his steaming cup.

"I could never do that," said Polly in a calm, steady voice. "How can you drink it so hot?"

Clarence grinned. "Asbestos tongue," he said gently, "neceselly (his imitation of a Chinese pronunciation was as absurd as Polly's own would be) for enjoyment of Chinese *haute cuisine*."

Polly chuckled. He was beginning to feel better, even relaxed. He was glad to be alone with Clarence, away from the busybodies upstairs. He left his tea steaming on the side before daring to sip it.

"Tell me, Clarence, how your family came to Hong Kong. Because you are Shanghainese, aren't you?"

"Oh, Mr Polly, how clever you are! You could tell from the swishing and slurring of my Cantonese pronunciation that I am a Northerner."

Polly smiled. "Don't be silly, Clarence," he said affectionately, "but go on, tell me the story, who came here first? Was it Grandpa Leo? And what made him leave Shanghai?"

"I will present some facts, Mr Polly, and then you have to decide if they amount to a history," said Clarence, with a grin.

"My grandfather worked in the French concession in Shanghai; in fact, he had been educated in Paris and both my great-uncles went to the Sorbonne. So there really was a French connection."

Clarence leaned forward, drinking more from his cup. Polly who had propped himself up, could see the smooth line of his curved back.

"Back home in Shanghai, they began by working for a French bank based on the Bund. As you know, all the big businesses were clustered along the front. Full of foreigners, of course. Obviously, their fluency in the language and contacts in Paris helped them land the jobs. I think that lasted a year or two, perhaps more. But then Grandpa Leo decided to join the Hong Kong & Shanghai Bank, the leading city institution. It was quite a leap up the scale; he obtained a leading post in the new firm which enabled him to buy a long lease on a grand house in Riviere Avenue. Tennis courts and a gang of servants in attendance, all that jazz. As you can imagine the rest of the family weren't going to be left out. They moved in quickly."

"That must have been unusual for a Chinese gentleman at that time," said Polly, "I mean to live in that part of the city, usually full of foreigners."

"What makes you assume he was a gentleman?" Clarence smirked. "Most gentlemen don't have four wives, but he did. Each one was installed in a different wing of the mansion. Very much Chinese style."

Polly smiled again. He wondered if Clarence was beginning to embroider the truth.

"Are you sure about the four wives, Clarence?" He enquired gently.

"Course I am," said Clarence in the exact offended tone of the English schoolboy he had been for twelve years.

"It's all a matter of face as usual for we Chinese. More wives, more sons, more face."

"Then what happened?" Polly asked.

"Then the Japanese came," said Clarence. "They invaded in 1941, you know that anyway. It had been expected, but in Shanghai-style, no one had done anything about it. I believe my aunties were playing *mahjong* when the planes roared over Riviere Avenue."

Polly imagined that elsewhere in Shanghai, in the Long Bar on the Bund, people had probably been settling down to a gin and tonic when the attack began. It would be the same in Hong Kong if the Chinese ever crossed the border; everyone would be at a cocktail party or at the races in Happy Valley. That would be the local version of Pompeii, people at the baths when Vesuvius erupted.

"Anyway, Grandpa Leo got away. The others didn't. I can tell you that the treatment they got in the hands of the Japanese was pretty barbaric," added Clarence.

He paused for a moment and suddenly turned to face Polly. Polly studied his face closely. He had a less triangular shape than that of many of his fellow countrymen. His eyes too were larger and more luminous than normal among the Chinese, at that moment they had a defiant, angry stare in them. His face was pale, in contrast to his exposed, tanned chest which was defined by a balanced muscularity. He was very handsome.

"That's why, Mr Polly, I hate them, the Japanese. They are fiendishly cruel; they are vulgar underneath all the pretended polish. And, like your lot, they are frightful imperialists."

There was a silence. Only the gentle lap of the water against the launch could be heard. There seemed to be no sound at all from above, on deck. Everyone, even the dean, must have collapsed in the midday heat. A seagull cried in the distance.

"Of course, I understand your bitterness, Clarence," Polly heard himself saying, annoyed that he sounded like a middle-of-the-way, liberal-pacifist academic.

"But it's not reasonable to hold a whole race responsible for the actions of a few butchers. Armies are trained to kill people and they get out of control. Look at what's gone on in China and is still going on—the great Chairman's hands are not bloodless."

"Rubbish," said Clarence vehemently, "you are wrong, Mr Polly, and that's why you will stay as you are, stuck in the History Department at Hong Kong

University, always an observer, a political eunuch, even when history is being made around you."

He reddened as he spoke. Polly guessed rightly that he had regretted his words as soon as he had uttered them. It was the first time Clarence had ever been rude to him. They were both embarrassed by his outburst.

"That's rather personal, Clarence," said Polly pleased at his own restraint, "in any case, the eunuchs were powerful folk in the Forbidden City."

Clarence did not answer. His expression had changed. His usual jocular facetiousness had evaporated like the steam coming from his teacup. He looked grim, he looked older. They sat in silence again.

"Look, Clarence," said Polly after a few minutes. "I'm not trying to minimise the suffering your family went through. I was just trying to get some perspective on it all. It must have been a terrifying experience."

Clarence did not seem to hear him. Instead, he began speaking again in a flat, monotonal voice.

"My grandfather and Mei-Mei, his youngest wife, or concubine if you prefer, managed to get out of the city. It was pandemonium. Tremendous panic and people struggling along the Bund, clutching cases; rickshaws still weaving through the crowds, everyone was fighting to get on board the few last ships that were leaving. Grandfather had large sums of money in cash which, like many Chinese, he kept at home. On that day he stuffed one of those school children's bamboo baskets full of notes. By bribing and threatening everyone in his way, he got on one of the ships and escaped. A few hours later, he would not have made it. Thousands didn't. Members of his own family disappeared and were never heard of again."

Polly waited a moment to let Clarence get over his emotions.

"And from there, where did they go?"

"They joined the mass exodus of the Chinese bourgeoisie who wandered from one city to another, first stop was Harbin. But as the Japanese advanced south, they had to move on until they ended up here in Hong Kong. But the Lams were a tough bunch; they were determined to make the new Shanghai wherever they landed up. On the way, they did whatever they could to survive. At one point my grandfather was even working in a circus; Mei-Mei danced on top of horses instead of bar tops. Can you imagine a man of my grandfather's background reduced to that? But they made it!"

"Quite a shock after life in Riviere Avenue," said Polly.

"And all the while," Clarence continued, as if not noticing Polly's remark at all, "thousands of our people were slaughtered by those yellow bastards."

Clarence's racist remark did not shock Polly. The Chinese always regarded themselves as superior to every other race. More surprisingly they considered themselves 'white', not the ruddy milky colour of Westerners, but snow white, like porcelain.

"And if they were not actually killed, they starved to death," Clarence added sombrely.

"And that's why Chairman Mao has such a following," said Polly, "because, at last, he stood up for the Chinese against all foreigners?"

"Exactly," said Clarence, "someone who would get them all out, for once and for all. That's why the party is supported by every true patriot."

Clarence stopped. Polly noticed, with relief that his expression had changed. He had got over his anger. Soon he would be completely composed; once more wearing the light-hearted mask that he seldom put aside.

"And of course, the people," he added with a sudden grin. "The people, and the people alone, are the motive force in the making of world history."

"I do recognise the quote, Clarence, and I could add all that stuff about the masses being the real heroes, but what do you think the chairman meant by 'world' history? The history of China?"

"You know jolly well, Mr Polly," said Clarence whose spirits were now quite restored, "that world history is a moment in the dialectic; it isn't trivial, provincial nonsense, like the gates of Kam Tin, with all respect to Uncle Eddie, but true history, Mr Polly. There is a true history of peoples and there is a true history of individuals."

Polly was intrigued.

"And does that apply to each of us?"

"To some of us, Mr Polly, to a chosen few. The vast majority will only share the true history of their people. But a few, you and I, we will have our own true history."

Perhaps it is frightening to have a true history of oneself thought Polly. He said aloud, "But how does one achieve one's true history?"

"In various ways," said Clarence, stressing the first syllable of 'various' in a sinister tone, "but you will know, Mr Polly. Like the prince well-advised, you will be the first to know."

Polly was enjoying Clarence's banter and would have been happy to continue talking to him in the same vein, but their privacy was interrupted by the crashing of heavy footsteps on the stairs leading down to the cabin. It was a red-faced Meissen, followed by Alistair Crowley, whose appearance looked uncharacteristically dishevelled.

"Everything alright?" Meissen said, then seeing Polly sitting up and obviously well, he went on, "Ah, you look quite restored, Polly, well done."

He gave Clarence a wink, then in a kindlier tone than Polly could remember for some time, he said, "Come up and get some fresh air, Polly. We are anchored now. The boat is quite still and they've put a great awning up against the sun. It will do you the world of good."

Polly nodded gratefully. So, everyone was pretending that his turn had been a touch of seasickness or sunstroke. Just as well.

"Thank you, Dean. I feel much better, the stomach's settled down," he said, patting himself and feeling a bit empty, "but it's a good idea to get some fresh air."

Clarence had already stood up and left the cabin. He was followed by Alistair Crowley who had kept silent, but whose expression was unsympathetic.

When the others had gone, Meissen spoke quietly.

"Polly, you've been under a lot of strain. Take a few days off. In fact, take the rest of the term off, if you like. There's nothing special coming up and there are only ten days left anyway. Hopkinson is back now so we can easily cover for you."

"Thank you, Dean, but it really isn't necessary. I am quite alright now."

He tried to keep the quavering tone out of his voice when he added, "You see, I get this occasional buzz, pressure on the ears or something and then it's gone."

"In the small circle of pain within the skull," quoted the dean.

"Well, I'm not planning martyrdom, Dean," said Polly, to show that he recognised the quotation. "Becket was a man of destiny."

"And you are a man of history, Polly, quite a different matter."

Polly did not answer.

"Come on, then, Polly," said the dean jovially, "let's go up before people think something has happened to me as well as you. It's almost teatime. By the way, Fiona is quite concerned about you."

Meissen turned on his heels and was bounding up the stairs. Polly followed at his pace, warmed at the thought of Fiona's concern.

When he reached the deck, he was surprised to find everything quiet and peaceful. One or two of the heartier launch-picnic guests had dived overboard, into the clear, green sea and had swum off towards the shore, with its golden-sanded beach, about a third of a mile away. Others were on the very top of the launch, on the exposed cabin roof, sunning themselves. A number had fallen asleep in deck chairs, exhausted by the heat and the Buck's Fizz. Walking quietly to the side, Polly suddenly saw Fiona Meissen, slumbering in a deck chair, head drooping to one side and mouth slightly ajar. In the midday heat, her lipstick had begun to run slightly, making it look as if blood was dripping out of her mouth. How odd to see her so unpoised, he thought.

At the end of the boat, Chief Inspector Chan was fishing, wearing a large straw hat to protect him from the glare. Alistair Crowley had also installed himself there, with a towel draped over his head like a shawl, reading a crumpled English newspaper. Clarence was nowhere to be seen.

Polly helped himself to some cold water from a glass bottle which had been kept cool, with other drinks, in an iced container hidden under the table. He tried to think of something arresting to say for his lecture the next day.

The events he was dealing with were dramatic enough. It was 1453. A young, handsome Sultan of twenty, Mehmed II entered the sanctum of Byzantium, a city known as the second Rome, with its vast treasures, public monuments and glittering palaces. The Sultan, mounted on a white charger, rode on until he reached the Cathedral of Holy Wisdom which the great Justinian, Roman Emperor, had built hundreds of years before. In front of that sacred, symbolic monument, he dismounted and picking some earth from the ground, threw it over his shoulder as an act of propitiation for Allah the Almighty.

And from that conquest, a new empire started. One in which many races mingled and many, like the Greeks and Armenians, would take their part in the affairs of the state. Centuries of statecraft, centuries of arts and merchant business would be practised. The state would thrive and expand in all directions; the lives of millions would be administered from the centre of a vast web, in that sanctum where the Conqueror now paused. How much had all this come about simply because of the wilful action of one man?

Polly considered the historical facts. All his life, Mehmed had nurtured the ambition to capture the city. In his European name, Edirne, as a young man, had dreamt of marching on the fabulous Constantinople and seizing it. He had made his plans carefully so that the city would be taken with the minimum of physical damage to its churches and monuments. He wanted the conqueror's spoils undamaged. In his waking hours, he thought of little else. Sitting in the airy courtyard of the palace interior at Edirne, learning his Greek words from a white-bearded, old tutor, his mind ever wandered towards his object, the city, the city that at all costs he had to conquer and which he would celebrate as a wise, cosmopolitan ruler.

So, the 'city of world desires' became the desire of one man. One strong, single-minded man, in a position to affect the course of history. The general and the particular thought Mr Polly, the course of events interrupted by a single will, or a single will be drawn into the general course of events? A greedy, ambitious man whose actions were part of a pattern, a series of causes and effects over which he had no control, or a man who actually changed that pattern. Was it credible to offer, as the historical explanation for the culmination of more than a thousand years of Byzantine history, the arrival of one individual at the gates of the city?

It wasn't going to be easy to get all this across in one lecture. Especially if Laura Li was present.

# Chapter 7

Polly's speculation was interrupted when a shadow fell over him as he sat on the open deck. It was Clarence again, refreshed from a long swim, the salty brine drying on his sleek skin. "A penny for your thoughts, Mr Polly," said Clarence in a friendly, relaxed tone, "whatever great thoughts they are."

"Nothing very much," said Polly defensively, "at any rate, nothing that is going to be settled this afternoon."

"Oh, the eternal verities," said Clarence, giving a good imitation of Anthony Bridges, "it is all too much for a simple, Chinese lad like me."

Polly grinned. Clarence was one of the last people he would have described as simple, but he let the remark pass. In any case, it was a relief that Clarence was once again his ebullient self and that all the anger that had surfaced when he was talking about his family fleeing from Shanghai had been tucked away. What other secrets were hidden under that smooth exterior? Polly wondered. Sometimes he had the feeling that Clarence was about to say something significant which he had hitherto kept silent about. Occasionally he felt that Clarence was probing him. Yet each time he seemed to stop short. Polly could not fathom what he wanted to find out.

"Clarence, I would like to go ashore. The island looks inviting and the sea is calm. Will you come with me?"

"Of course," said Clarence, "bit of guidance from the natives and a bit of interpreting, perhaps. I'll do my best with these idle Southerners, these Cantonese."

Polly got up and reached for his straw hat. Luckily, everyone on deck was either reading or asleep so they would not be joined by anyone. He needed to escape from the others and from any further questioning about his behaviour. He followed Clarence to the rear of the vessel where a small rowing boat was suspended in the air. He heard Clarence rousing the crew, who had been enjoying their well-earned siesta, and he wondered why the Cantonese always sounded as if they were arguing when they spoke. It was the guttural sounds of the language. But they responded, relieved when Clarence told them that there was no need for them to accompany him and Polly ashore. He would manage the boat. They just needed to get it down into the water. Soon it was being lowered and Polly enjoyed the noise of the splash as it hit the water, calm and quite translucent.

"Come on then," said Clarence, who had already hopped aboard, "no time for deliberation, Mr Crusoe, your deserted island beckons."

Polly did not jump. It was a pity; he reflected that he was not a person for taking leaps either of a physical or metaphysical nature. Instead, he climbed over the railings of the launch rather awkwardly and tried to steady himself by putting one foot on the boat first, nervous that his sandals would make him slip. Clarence, seeing his hesitation, held out a steady hand which Polly gripped as he swung his other leg onto the planks of the small boat.

"Right," said Clarence, "let's go," and with a deft tug, started the engine of the little boat which roared off bobbing up and down in the water. Soon they were speeding along, Clarence seated on the stern, captain-like, with the ensign flapping behind him.

As they approached land, he shouted out enthusiastically:

"The beach is marvellous, let's get ashore as soon as we can." Then he cut the engine off and let the boat drift inwards towards the shore. Soon it hit the shallow sands.

"Take your shoes and socks off, Mr Polly, because we have to wade from here. Look you can see the white sand at the bottom, wrinkled in little patterns by the current."

The silence was wonderful, once the engine was off. The only sound to be heard was the water lapping against the side of the boat and the noise of splashing as Clarence jumped into the shallow water and began to pull it further in. A lone dog barked in the distance. Polly breathed deeply, what an escape from the mad bustle of Hong Kong; what a joy to get away from the babble of words and the clink of glasses that made up its unending social rounds. Polly unbuckled his sandals, then peeled off the brilliant red socks which he had worn deliberately to annoy Alistair Crowley. Nothing like caricaturing oneself. Rolling up both trouser bottoms, he put his feet into the blissfully warm water, seeing his toes on the surface of the sand below the water and small, transparent miniature crabs scurrying off. There was a delicious softness on the soles of his feet as he paddled towards the shore, with the ripples of gentle waves in front of him.

If it were my fate to expire at this minute, he caught himself thinking—it was a thought that came to him now and again and one that he usually dismissed as soon as it arose—there could be worse endings. The quiet, the water and the feeling of peace were perfect preparations for the longest journey. But his morbid turn of thought was interrupted by a cry from Clarence who was clambering up the rocks to the side of the beach.

"Come up here, sir. There's a path that goes up into the hills. Let's go up to the top and find the small farm I've visited before. It's simple and rustic. Spirit of Confucius and all that: come on, Mr Polly, you'll be amused."

Getting into his sandals again, Polly panted up the hill behind the agile Clarence who always seemed to have jumped up to the next level just as he thought he had caught up with him. Polly's heart was pounding, the sweat poured from him, and he began to think that expiring down on the gentle sands of the beach may not have been a bad option. It felt as if, step by step, they were climbing a steep mountain, but when he paused for breath and looked down, it was no great distance they had covered after all. By now, his ankles had been stung by insects and a kind of prickly gorse had caught on his sandals, scratching the bare skin of his leg. He had been bitten, unbelievably, on his head, despite the fact that he was wearing a hat.

At length, he caught up with Clarence who, without any sign that he had lost breath, was waiting for him on a ledge covered in wild mimosa. Polly took in the beauty of the flowers, but he was too hot to comment. In any case, Clarence would have noticed; he saw everything.

"Come on, sir," he said, springing forwards and then, to encourage Polly, "we are almost there."

They made the rest of the ascent in silence, only the sound of the dragonflies buzzing past. Polly murmured:

*The dragonfly and bumblebee*
*Hummed dreams of paradise to thee.*

"John Clare," said Clarence in his bright-as-a-button, know-it-all manner. "I did a brief term in English under Prof B who virtually invented Clare, didn't he?" He smirked.

"Well, brought him to light," said Polly, "poor, poor Clare."

"But terrible spelling," Clarence went on, "jolly difficult for us natives to follow, you know, all that dialect stuff."

The two men now stood shoulder to shoulder at the top of the hill high up from the bay. Looking down the rocky edges to the beach and across the green, glistening water, they could see the launch rolling slightly at anchor, looking far out, with its white bow gleaming in the sun. It was early evening and just beginning to cool off slightly.

"Now what would Clare have made of this," said Clarence, "if he had been transported from that green English countryside? Would he have been able to cope?"

Polly did not reply. He wondered how Clarence had coped, spending all those years cooped up in an English public school, taken away from his natural environment. And now he seemed so anglicised, at least on the surface.

"Come and meet Ah Sung, the farmer," said Clarence. "Don't mind about the dogs. They sound ferocious, but they are tied up."

Clarence walked ahead until they reached a small clearing which was hidden from view behind the rocks. The black, husky guard dogs had stopped barking but stood, tied up in the shade, snarling. A few straggly chickens pecked at the dust. Polly could hear the raised, excited voices of young children, as they played, in the background. Mr Sung came out to greet his uninvited guests, giving them a courteous bow and motioning them to enter his house, a flimsy bamboo structure that had nevertheless survived the lashings of numerous typhoons. Inside the hut, there was a single dark room which Polly found quite airless, and which gave out a pungent, earthy smell mingled with something smoky. The only air coming in was through the front door which Mr Sung had left wide open.

As they entered and sat down on hard, traditional wooden stools, Clarence muttered something in Cantonese to Mr Sung who beamed broadly revealing a row of gold-filled teeth.

"I've told him that you are a distinguished scholar, Mr Polly. You know that among Chinese, especially the illiterate classes, all learning is venerated, so you become a guest with a special status. Mrs Sung will be back in a moment with tea."

Polly nodded. His eyes had now adjusted to the darkened atmosphere of the room. Looking around him, he could see that it was very simply furnished with some tattered flowery curtains to the side almost concealing a tiny window. In the corner, a makeshift altar on which stood a bowl filled with sand and burning joss sticks. There was very little furniture, but a few small wooden benches which the visitors sat on. From the back area, cordoned off with some hanging beads, Mrs Sung emerged clutching a tin tray with three small bowls and a white pot, decorated with garish chrysanthemums. She put them on the small, round table in front of the three men and withdrew without saying a word.

Mr Sung poured out the tea and without waiting for it to cool, picked up his bowl and inclining his head towards Polly, proposed a toast.

"He is wishing you, learned gentleman, much luck in the future. Good food and many… sons, actually," said Clarence blushing.

"Well, how kind," said Polly, "you must return the compliment if that is not considered rude."

Clarence spoke again in Cantonese and Mr Sung beamed even more broadly. There was then a moment's silence as it seemed no one quite knew what to say. Outside, the sun was beginning to set, lending a glow to the hillside.

Mrs Sung reappeared to take the teapot away for refilling. With a strange gurgling noise, Mr Sung began to speak again. Polly caught the word for storm, literally 'big wind'.

"Mr Sung is saying," said Clarence, "that there is going to be another typhoon. It's coming across the sea and he thinks it will hit the island within forty-eight hours."

"But that's incredible," said Polly, "there's been nothing about it on the weather report. How does he know?"

Clarence mumbled to Mr Sung in a rapid drawl.

Mr Sung smiled; he seemed pleased to be consulted about something that he did know about. It compensated for the learnedness which he recognised in his guests. Being in position to instruct educated people gave him a face. He sipped some tea before replying. When he had finished speaking, Clarence said to Polly.

"He says that one can tell by the smell of the wind and by the behaviour of animals, especially the pigs."

"How odd," said Polly, "but what sort of behaviour?"

"It's a bit rude," said Clarence evasively.

"Oh, come on," said Polly. "I'm not an innocent schoolboy."

"They are seldom innocent," joked Clarence, "at least not Chinese ones."

"You're dodging the point," said Polly, "come on, out with it."

"Well, Mr Sung says that the animals start doing odd things to each other. Unnatural sex."

Polly burst into laughter and to keep him company so did Mr Sung. At that very moment, Mrs Sung arrived back with the fresh tea and seeing the two men laughing, she grinned as well, although quite unaware, as indeed was her husband, of the cause of the merriment.

Noticing that Clarence did not seem to be amused, Polly stopped abruptly, wondering if he had caused offence. He had been in the Orient long enough to know that Mr Sung's laughter meant nothing; it was just a form of politeness. But Clarence's expression was no longer relaxed.

Suddenly Mr Sung got up and with a slight bow, disappeared to the back of the room.

"I think we had better be going soon," began Clarence, but before he could go on, Mr Sung had returned, clutching a small parcel wrapped neatly in old newspapers. He resumed the squatting position which he knew the *gweilo* would not be able to do. Slowly, Mr Sung unwrapped the parcel, peeling the layers off carefully, as if he were performing a religious rite. As the last piece of paper was removed, Polly could see, to his great surprise, a porcelain English egg coddler, with its distinctive Wedgwood hallmark.

Mr Sung beamed with pride and handed the object to Mr Polly for inspection. While Mr Polly was turning it round and doing his best to pretend that he was admiring it, Mr Sung spoke in Cantonese to Clarence.

"Mr Sung says that this object was given to him by the district officer when he retired ten years ago." He paused, and then added as an aside, "Can you imagine a more ridiculous gift?"

Polly smiled politely and carefully handed back Mr Sung the egg coddler. Glancing at it with pride once more, the old farmer began to wrap it up again in the layers of newspaper.

"Not very practical," said Polly to Clarence, keeping a pleasant tone in his voice. But to Mr Sung, he said in his best Cantonese, "*Ho laing*, very pretty, *ho laing.*"

"Anyway, time to go," said Clarence.

"This will take a few minutes. Let's begin the thanks to Mr Sung. He will thank us. Then we will thank him again. Then he will say that it has been an honour and so on. Eventually, we will be able to leave."

Polly was relieved. He had started to feel queasy. The heavy atmosphere inside the hut and the green tea on an empty stomach (with only the morning's Buck's Fizz in it) contributed to his feeling of being unwell. Their exhausting clamber up the hill had not helped. Even so, he felt that more than mere civilities were being exchanged as the two Chinese men talked on.

At last, Clarence got up; they all gave a final, farewell bow. Polly stumbled into the fresh air outside the hut, with some relief. The dogs, who had been quiet, leapt up again and began their chorus of snarling as if to make sure that the guests went off the premises as they should do. The two men walked down the hill at a reasonable pace and Polly, now feeling a good deal better, decided to tackle Clarence.

"I don't believe that you translated everything that Mr Sung said," he ventured as they paused on the ledge that gave a commanding view of the bay. Polly noticed that a great cluster of rocks lying on the beach when they had arrived now formed an island in the water. Their boat was still tied up, but further out than it had been, while the Lam launch seemed far away in the distance. The tide was turning and they would be wise to get back to the launch. He was surprised that Meissen had not sent out a search party, but then remembered that the boat they came on was the only one attached to the launch.

Clarence did not answer at once. He seemed pensive. He began to descend on the path again, with Polly a few steps behind.

"It's nothing, really, Mr Polly. After all, the man is only a farmer, an ignorant peasant."

"But what did he say," insisted Polly, trying to keep the irritation he felt out of his voice, "if it's not important, then what's the harm in telling me?"

There was another silence. Clarence picked up a piece of bamboo that had broken off a desiccated tree which they stood next to. Then he flung it back on the ground. Clarence cleared his throat.

"Well, if you must know he said you smelt like a devil, a foreigner. You brought the smell of burning with you."

Polly stopped in his tracks. He tried to catch Clarence's expression, but Clarence deliberately avoided looking at him. He felt awkward and at the same time ruffled.

"I suppose that's an example of the respect you were saying that the Chinese have for scholars," he blurted out sarcastically, regretting his outburst at once.

Clarence reddened, but he did not reply. Instead, he continued down the steep path, flattening the earth with his foot in places so it would be easier for Polly to follow him. Polly looked around him, the dragonflies were still buzzing. Then he gazed upwards, into the still clear sky over his head, noticing that in the distance it was dark and threatening. The atmosphere had become oppressively still, he felt himself sweating at the bottom of his back, just above his belt. He began to clamber down again, landing his feet in the places that Clarence had clearly stamped out for him. Soon he felt his bare soles sink into the delicious hot sand of the beach. Clarence was sitting under the shade of a tree, but Polly did not join him.

"Perhaps we should be getting back to the launch," he said, "in case Mr Sung's weather forecasting is better than Rediffusion's."

Clarence nodded and got up, wading out to pull the boat nearer to shore so that Polly could get aboard more easily.

# Chapter 8

The two Englishmen, slightly red-faced, were another pair of *gweilos* or foreign devils crossing Hankow Road on a sultry afternoon. They stood out a mile among the sleek and svelte Cantonese, an easy target for Ah Lap, the street-seller who had been following their progress from the moment they left the restaurant. He sold everything from cheap cotton shirts to smiling, rotund Buddhas, made of sandstone.

Rushing after them, he shouted out, "Vely special plice," unfolding a great cloth which revealed a row of gleaming watches.

"No thank you, very much," said Anthony Bridges winking at Polly, "they look as if they have come from a very special place. On we go."

Ah Lap pursues them down the street.

"No stealing, mister, my blother in the business."

"Yes, I'm sure he's in the business, as you say, but we don't want them. Go away! *Jow*!"

The hawker backed a sour look on his face. Foreign devils, that's all they are, he thought to himself, nothing but well-fed barbarians who could easily afford one of his gleaming watches. They should spend a day on the streets to see how they would feel after it. He gave up following them.

As they walked along, Polly revived their previous conversation.

"Do you know more than you let on," said Polly when they had escaped the vendor's attentions, "I mean about the political situation?"

"Not really," said Anthony Bridges, panting in his attempt to talk as well as keep pace with Polly.

"But just look at the facts dispassionately. Across the border from Lo Wu, there are said to be over a hundred thousand Chinese Red Army troops. And behind them, any number of reserve battalions. All highly disciplined professionals ready for action at a moment's notice. And what have we got? Ten thousand soldiers, unused to the tropical heat, and some keen volunteers? What are they going to be able to do faced with that force?"

"But wouldn't a Chinese invasion here provoke a war? What about the Americans?"

"Oh, no doubt Alistair Crowley will tell you that the Yanks are obliged to come in. But it's all nonsense. Even if it's true that they would come to the rescue, they are based in Taiwan. How long would that take? It would all be over by the time they arrived."

"So, the Chinese could take us over at any time?" Polly said, feeling he was committing an act of treason by just uttering the words.

"Of course, they could," said Anthony Bridges with a smirk. "Just a day's work. But don't say that in front of Crowley. He'll have you locked up for high treason."

They were now at the great doors of the Peninsula Hotel which were flung open at once by two bell-boys in their immaculate white uniforms and round hats.

"I find Crowley a bit sinister," said Polly, as they entered the grand foyer, with its great columns and throne-like chairs placed at stately intervals beneath them.

"Very Colonial Office," said Anthony Bridges puffing a little as they walked up the grand staircase to the first floor. "Doesn't have much time for the chattering classes and even less for us in academe."

Glancing round the almost empty lounge, he pointed to a corner near the French doors.

"Ah, there's a good nook, let's sit there."

"Now what will you have, G&T or pink g?"

"I'll have a San Miguel," said Polly who knew he could never keep up with Anthony Bridges' drinking.

"Boy," called out Anthony to a waiter standing nearby, "a large gin and tonic and one San Mig."

Then to Polly, he said, "Excuse me, Polly, duty calls, be back in a moment."

Left alone in the comfortable, spacious room with its luxurious vast sofas, gilt-edged tables and elegant, long velvet curtains, Polly did not feel relaxed. In fact, he felt excited; his heart was beating faster. Lower down, he could feel something stirring. He raised himself slightly from his seat, without actually getting up, to survey the area around the large doors, which were wide open and looked out onto the front, canopied terrace. To the left of the windows, there was an elegant, tall palm in a fine blue and white bowl raised on a lacquered jardiniere, next to that a small writing table, in Blackwood, with a stylish bamboo wastepaper basket underneath. Polly got up from his chair to have a closer look. The wastepaper basket was full of uncollected paper. Excellent! That was the place he thought with deliberate calculation, that is the place to start the fire.

Suddenly, Polly felt that he was being watched. Anthony Bridges had come back from behind him, stopped in the middle of the room and must have been staring at Polly for some moments. His timing suggested that he wanted Polly to realise that he was being watched.

"I didn't see you there, old boy," said Polly a little breathlessly.

Anthony Bridges faced Polly without speaking for a moment. Then he said in a quite unsympathetic voice, "What are you doing, Polly?"

"Nothing special," said Polly ignoring the hostility in his colleague's tone. "Just having a look outside on the terrace," he added, realising how unconvincing he sounded.

"I really think…" began Anthony Bridges but stopped himself from saying whatever he had intended to say. Instead, he did not sit down, but reaching for his glass, emptied its contents with a gulp. He spoke slowly, in a flat monotone, "Jolly nice occasion, Polly, but I've got to go."

The expression on his face was grim; all traces of good humour had vanished from it. With a curt nod, he strode across the room to the bar where he signed a chit for the bill. A sleek member of staff appeared with his Panama hat. Anthony Bridges took it from the attendant and still holding it in his hand, marched out of the room without looking back.

Polly realised that the whole thing had been planned. Anthony Bridges had deliberately left him alone in the room so as to be able to spy on him. But what had made him do it? The image of Chief Inspector Chan flashed before him. It had been clear from the time of the incident with Clarence that Anthony Bridges was closely in touch with the chief inspector. It began to look like an elaborate conspiracy.

Alone once again, Polly sipped his beer slowly. For the first time, he noticed that the light buzzing noise had returned to his head. He rocked his head from side to side, like a swimmer who had emerged from the water with his ears blocked. But it had no effect: the buzz was still there. Polly looked around the room which was now quite deserted. He got up and walked to the window, standing near the curtain. He began to edge the wastepaper bin out, with his foot, from under the table so that it was right up against the curtain. Then he felt in his pocket for the highly inflammable ball that he had hidden there. Suddenly there was a noise. Polly froze; he could hear his heart beating. A waiter walked past, balancing a large silver tray with drinks on it. In another moment, he had gone onto the terrace.

Polly pulled the packet out of his pocket, threw it in the bin and quick as lightning, took out a box of matches, lit one and threw it onto the bundle which immediately ignited violently. Then he turned on his heels, forcing himself to walk slowly out of the bar without looking back. He proceeded down the grand staircase quickly without actually rushing; when he reached the bottom he turned to the right, passing along the arcaded foyer. His heart was pounding.

# Chapter 9

When Polly walked out of the Peninsula Hotel, the sun had disappeared. Although it was only three in the afternoon, the sky was dark. There was a strange stillness in the air. Polly felt breathless as he crossed Hankow Road and walked into the YMCA, pushing its revolving entrance doors. He made his way straight to the toilets, to the side, on the ground floor with their small slats giving onto the busy Salisbury Road. No one was inside. Polly went into a cubicle, locking himself in. Hardly had he got there when he heard, from outside, the roar of noise as the fire engines came blaring down the main road, causing all the traffic to pull over. Polly sank down and unbuttoned his trousers…

Polly had no idea how long he had been in the cubicle. He had lapsed into a trance, noticing that the buzzing in his head had stopped. He tried to remember when that had happened, but he could not be precise. Every other event of the last half-an-hour, however minute, was stamped on his mind. But he had not noticed exactly when the buzzing had stopped. Polly turned the toilet roll, tore off a strip and began cleaning himself. As he pulled up his trousers, he heard the door of the toilets open and someone come in. He would wait, he thought, a few minutes until they had gone. He stood still, listening. There was complete silence. Polly waited for a little while; then he decided that he should come out of the cubicle. When he opened the door, he saw a man at the urinal with his back towards him. All was well. Polly walked towards the wash basins, ran some water and began to wash his hands. The man at the urinal did not move. Polly dried his hands on the towel and turned towards the door.

At that moment, the man at the urinal turned to face him. To Polly's consternation, it was Chief Inspector Chan who spoke calmly.

"Mr Polly, please don't say anything. Listen to what I have to say. You can't escape from here. My men are outside the door and at all the entrances and exits to this building. I would like you to come with me to Tsim Sha Shui Police Station for questioning. If you do as I say, it will be a moderately civilised affair.

If you don't, I will be forced to arrest you here and now and you will be led out in handcuffs."

Polly froze on the spot. Ideas flashed through his mind. He remembered the last time he had spoken to the chief inspector on the launch picnic to Lamma Island. What could have been more idyllic, the cerulean sea, the somnolent afternoon, the idle chatter and splendid food? How safe and secure! Clarence to look after him when he had felt unwell, the solicitous, pretty eyes of Fiona Meissen looking at him with kindly concern. And now, what a contrast. He was in a situation of utter sordidness, the worldly chief inspector waiting for him to decide, waiting for him to condemn himself to further humiliation. How could these events have happened? It seemed as if they were happening to someone else.

Chief Inspector Chan interrupted his thoughts.

"Good," he said, "let's go quietly."

He moved towards Polly, and then said with his hand on the door, "When we walk out of here, just follow me. Two of my chaps will fall in behind us. If you make a move or do anything silly, they will go for you. Be careful, Mr Polly, they are burly Northerners, Shantung boys, who would think nothing of breaking a man's arm. None of this delicate, Cantonese stuff."

Chief Inspector Chan's remark, with its bantering, but sinister undertone, struck Polly forcibly and brought him painfully back to reality. For the first moment since Anthony Bridges had walked out on him in the bar at the Peninsula, he began to look for a balance in things; he began to realise that no matter how ghastly the situation he was in, however grotesque, there would be some lighter aspects, even perhaps something of interest to be gleaned from it. Life was full of surprises. The yin and the yang. And he knew that he was dealing with a clever, sophisticated man who would carry out whatever duties he had to do in a civilised manner, with humour and courtesy. After all, they were in the East, no one took a high moral line on the foibles of their fellows; it was a matter of supreme indifference to the chief inspector whether Polly was normal or abnormal, morally at fault or not, whether he had scruples or none.

Chief Inspector Chan was concerned only with the public consequences of Polly's behaviour. He was concerned with him, thought Polly, in the way that he, Polly, was concerned with the characters of history. He might probe, dissect and analyse in order to understand, in order to decide what account to give of Polly's behaviour and how to deal with him for the good of society. He would need to gather facts that he saw as being material to this quest, selecting what was significant and discarding what he judged irrelevant. In putting together these facts, he would hope to arrive at a judicious judgement about what to do. But he did all this in a detached spirit, just as detached as Polly was when he was studying his favourite Ottoman Grand Vizier. The chief inspector was not out to judge him. Polly need have no fear on that account.

By now Polly was seated next to Chief Inspector Chan in the police jeep. He felt a little dizzy; he was completely parched. They were driving up the steep and surprisingly leafy road (it reminded Polly of an English country lane) to the police station, secreted on a verdant hilltop in the midst of the sprawl of urban Kowloon. A heat haze hung over the city; the air was oppressive. Chief Inspector Chan was smoking a Turkish cigarette but was careful not to blow the smoke in the direction of Polly.

"You know the thing I miss most about England," he said, breaking the silence, "is the English countryside."

He stressed the last syllable of the word.

"Not your neat, trim southern counties either," he continued, "but something more rugged. You know that I went to school in Yorkshire, like Clarence. From time to time, we were let out, so to speak, and we would go up to Northumberland, to the moors and along the lovely, desolate coast. It was the only time we could ever be alone, far from the madding crowd."

Polly reflected on the bizarre quirk of empire. Here he was, on a sweltering afternoon in a distant colony in the South China Sea, headed towards a police station for interrogation and what was the subject of conversation—the Northumberland coast! A coast that this Chinaman knew far better than he, a native-born Englishman, but a mere Southerner. Of course, Polly understood that Chief Inspector Chan was making his opening gambit in what was going to be a complicated game of chess. Polly would have to be clever. The chief inspector was being much civilised, but he would bargain. He wanted something in return.

"Well, the northeast is not everyone's choice," Polly replied, "a little bleak, some would say."

"Life itself can be bleak, Mr Polly," said the chief inspector and whether his tone had become more sinister or whether Polly had just imagined it, there was no time to decide for the jeep had swung through the gates and onto the gravel path that ran up to the old, colonial building, shaded by some trees, its brown shutters half-closed against the sun. The chief inspector acknowledged a salute from the constable on guard duty by raising the end of his cane to the hat. In moments, they had screeched to a halt and the policemen quickly jumped out of the vehicle.

"Follow the constable up to my office," said Chief Inspector Chan to Polly. "I will catch you up in a few minutes."

They entered the dark, cool building with its red-tiled floor, but instead of making for the charge room straight ahead, they marched down a side corridor and up a flight of steps to the first floor. On the walls which they passed, photos of the station's personnel from different years beamed out at them. Most of them were red-faced colonials. The constable opened the half-glass door marked 'Chief Inspector' and motioned Polly to go in. Immaculate in his khaki uniform, the young policeman said politely in punctilious English, "You may sit down, sir, but please don't leave this room."

Polly sank into a rattan chair, facing the desk. Suddenly he felt extremely weak. He was dehydrated and the excitement of the last hour was now catching up with him. He looked around. The room was comfortable for an office; it even exuded a touch of luxury. The chief inspector's desk was of gleaming rosewood. On it stood a shaded table lamp, a black telephone and a pile of papers, neatly stacked in a tray that was marked 'Immediate'. Behind his chair, which was finely carved and rounded in the Ming style, there was a standing lamp, whose stem twirled in the shape of a dragon. On the walls were faded, framed photographs of early Hong Kong scenes, showing the tiny cluster of buildings on the harbour front in the 1860s. In one corner a college photo with a young, but recognisable Eddie Chan, in a smart blazer and college tie, grinning broadly in the front row. Underneath, a small brass plaque marked 'Balliol College, Oxford, 1934'.

The chief inspector reappeared, motioning Polly to stay where he was.

"Would you like a drink, Mr Polly, you must be tired from the heat?" He said without the slightest hint of irony in his voice.

"A glass of water would be welcome," Polly answered.

The chief inspector pressed a button in a small round bell on his desk. A moment later, a constable opened the door and quickly saluted. Chief Inspector Chan muttered in Cantonese; as the constable withdrew he started re-arranging the papers on his desk.

"Always taught to be methodical, Mr Polly," he chuckled, "but then I hardly have to tell you, a distinguished historian, and such an obvious thing."

He pulled out a paper from the pile that was in front of him and appeared to be reading it.

Polly remained silent. He marvelled at the chief inspector's good humour. What a subtle, Oriental way to do things. The door swung open and the constable re-entered with a tray. There was a jug of water and ice, as well as two large bottles of cold San Miguel beer, the mist rising from them.

"We may need something stronger than water as we progress," said the chief inspector, "but let's begin with the water."

Leaning back in his throne-like chair, he sipped from his glass.

"Let's see. You are Augustus John Polly, aged 38, born in Beckenham, Kent, educated at Tonbridge Grammar School and London University. Married to Maud Manderley-Simpson. Divorced after a short period, I see. Is all that correct?"

Polly nodded. How brutally short a life can be made. How misleadingly bland are the lines of any CV or record? Simple words—married to Maud Manderley-Simpson; divorced. A few words to cover a whole mess of emotion and involvement, thick, sickeningly vicious emotional entanglement, embarrassing, ugly details. And the mess and the pain of it all, and the cost. Scenes that Polly would prefer to forget, but could not, even ten thousand miles away at the other end of the earth. All summarised in a short phrase. Married to Maud Manderley-Simpson; divorced.

"Now at SEAS…"

"SOAS," interrupted Polly.

"Forgive me, Mr Polly, these colleges with acronyms don't come easily to an Oxford man. At SOAS," (he intoned the 'o' in the well-rounded way of well-educated foreigners), "you began to study history, or to be more specific, Ottoman history."

"Well, I came on to that," said Polly, "after my first year, I began to specialise in that area."

"Yes, indeed," said the chief inspector. "And was it at that time too that you first joined the Communist party?"

Polly started up. How had they discovered this? He did not know that his membership had been recorded anywhere.

"I joined the Student Marxist-Leninist Society," he said, then added as casually as he could, "everyone did."

"And was it about this time that you also began to be interested in Zoroastrianism?"

"Yes," said Polly, only too aware of the direction that the chief inspector's questioning was taking.

"One could not study Persian history without understanding it."

"Of course," said Chief Inspector Chan. "Alexander the Great and all that. But was that the only reason for your interest in it? What else did you find attractive about this obscure Persian religion?"

Polly tried not to flinch.

"I traced its survival in the Gabar communities, the way that…"

"Now, look here," said the chief inspector interrupting him, "let's not be silly. Zarathustra spoke of fire-worship, didn't he? That is what it was all about?"

"That was certainly one aspect of it," said Polly evasively.

"And it was the one that most interested you," said the chief inspector, his voice sounding stern. "Veneration of fire."

Polly did not answer.

"It seems to me," continued the chief inspector, "that you have at least two vices. One is a silly, venial one—you know that we Chinese don't care about sexual practices provided someone is producing the next generation. But the other matter, shall we call it your proclivity, that is more serious, potentially very awkward, to say the least."

"What are you accusing me of?" Polly said, tired of the shadow-boxing.

"I am saying, Mr Polly, that you have inherited the vice of your eponymous hero, HG Wells' character. We know that you admired him."

"I admired Wells' writing," said Mr Polly, trying to regain some lost ground, "and if I shared something of his socialism, so what? We've had a long stint of Labour Government, you know, and the world didn't end."

"No indeed," said the chief inspector, "I never disliked Major Attlee myself, such a reassuringly conservative figure. Still, it won't do you much good airing such views in Hong Kong or with…" He paused a moment, sipping his water, then finished, "Alistair Crowley and his brigade."

"There are lots of things I don't share with that brigade, as you call them," said Polly, trying not to be ruffled.

"Quite," said the chief inspector, suddenly leaning forward and ringing the bell again.

Within moments, the young policeman had come back and without a word, flipped off the metal caps of the two bottles of San Miguel beer with the opener that was lying next to them. While he carefully tipped the glasses and poured the beer, Polly caught a whiff of his starched khaki uniform. The glasses glistened with the still-cold liquid. The constable handed the two men a glass each and then withdrew.

Chief Inspector Chan sipped his beer. He motioned Polly to do the same. When he put his glass down again, he looked straight at Polly.

"Mr Wells' hero, as you know, decided to burn down the company business in order to collect the insurance. Now tell me why you tried to set fire to the Peninsula Hotel?"

Polly said nothing. He was beginning to feel unwell; there was a slight buzzing in his ears. He shifted in his seat, sticking to everything as he moved.

"I'm not feeling very well," he blurted out, "can you open the windows for some fresh air, it's awfully warm in here?"

"I could," said the chief inspector, "but at this time of day, that would increase rather than diminish the temperature. Here," he said, throwing Polly a damp cloth, "try this, a damp face cloth, Cantonese cure for everything. Have a *maat sum*, or wipe down, it might help."

Polly took the damp towel and sunk his face into it, holding himself in that position for a few moments. The cloth smelled faintly of Dettol. He tried to wipe the back of his neck where his shirt was sticking unpleasantly.

Chief Inspector Chan drained the rest of his beer and then wiped his own hands on a cloth.

"On this occasion, Mr Polly, nothing serious has happened. Your behaviour was noticed and reported to me—don't ask me by whom—you are not here to take part in a quiz."

Polly remembered the grim expression on Anthony Bridge's face as he had left him so abruptly in the bar.

"Suffice it to say that we got to the scene quickly and everything was under control before anything serious happened. The damage to the bar was minimal, about $500. I look forward to receiving that amount from you, Mr Polly, in cash, if you please, in cash. The hotel will take no further action."

Polly wondered how the chief inspector had stopped the hotel from pursuing him. The Lam/Chan network no doubt.

For a moment, the chief inspector seemed jovial.

"That's how we sort things out in Hong Kong," he said, with a grin. But suddenly his tone changed.

"But this will be the last time, Mr Polly. If you are ever involved in anything like this again—and beware, Mr Polly, we will be watching you—then you will be arrested and charged. I dare say that will be the end of your career. Do you understand what I am saying?"

Polly did not reply at once. He sensed an immediate, post-orgiastic kind of relief. So, he was not being charged. His pleasant world, his safe world which was only made unsafe by his own folly, would remain. Ah Hing would continue to annoy him; Dean Meissen would continue to bully him; he could still admire Ah Tang's body while pondering on the meaning of history. He knew he was expected to make a token remark.

"I'm grateful to you, Chief Inspector," he eventually managed to cough out, feeling some humiliation when he contemplated the impeccable performance that Chief Inspector Chan had put up.

"Good," said the chief inspector, "it is important that you have understood me clearly. And now, before you go, I suggest we have another beer and I can ask you about some historical questions that I've been storing up since the launch picnic."

Forty-five minutes later, Polly found himself walking along the steep road from the police station, lined with its pink hibiscus that seemed in continuous flower. Eddie Chan had offered him a lift to the Star Ferry but Polly had declined. A walk was just what he needed to clear his head. He looked at the elegant Swiss watch on his wrist. It had been given to him by a wealthy student who had graduated with honours the previous year. It was five-thirty.

When he reached the bottom of the road, Polly turned left and once again passed along the front of the YMCA until he reached the side-entrance to the Peninsula Hotel. The doorman gave him a salute, causing Polly a moment of hesitation. But of course, the man would salute him—he would any European who happened to be coming into the hotel. Or was the doorman's salute a fantastic gesture of Oriental inscrutability? Was he only too well aware of who Polly was, what he had been doing, and the magnanimous behaviour of Chief Inspector Chan who, after all, must have got the hotel to co-operate somehow? Could it be that all the staff had been warned against him, had been given a description of him with details of what the chief inspector had called his two vices?

Anything was possible thought Polly, brushing his way past the doorman and into the arcade that led along the side of the building. In any case, he was not going to go upstairs, into the bar again. He was not going to return to the scene of his crime where everything had been restored and there was not the slightest trace that anything untoward had happened. Instead of turning to the great staircase, Polly marched through the arcade of shops, dazzled by the brightly-lit windows with their jewels and passed the glittering Hong Kong Airways office with its glamorous Eurasian staff. He did not know why he had walked through the hotel at all. In a few minutes, he stepped out onto the thronging pavement of Nathan Road.

He crossed the road and walked along one of the arched arcades until he reached a small bar called 'Jingles'. He stood outside for a moment and then decided to enter. The place was almost deserted. An American sailor, in a crisp white uniform, was at one end of the bar, a forest of empty beer bottles in front of him. In one of the chairs, an older man in a slightly crumpled linen suit was slumped over a pink gin, apparently oblivious to the world.

Polly took a seat at the empty end of the bar and ordered himself a double scotch. Remembering that he still had *Vathek* in his pocket, he plucked it out, finding himself nearly at the end of the tale. He read.

*Thus, the Caliph Vathek, who, for the sake of empty pomp*
*and forbidden power, had sullied himself with a*
*thousand crimes, became a prey to grief without end,*
*and remorse without mitigation...*

He closed the book and picked up his drink, looking around the bar. A pair of effeminate Eurasian boys, still in their teens by the looks of it, had come in and were giggling. He could see that they were looking at him. Moments later, Polly received an unordered drink. On the tray next to it were scribbled some Latin words—*Nitimur in vetitum semper*, we always strive for the forbidden. Polly looked up and saw the two young men staring at him. Suddenly he recognised them as first-year students in the Classics Department. As he looked at them, the outline of their image became blurred. Polly could hear a buzzing noise in his head. Stumbling as he got up, Polly lunged towards the door, almost strangling himself on the jangling beads which hung at the entrance. He fell gasping into the blinding heat of Nathan Road.

# Chapter 10

A day or two later as he was walking past the comprador, Ah Chueng's shop, Polly looked down at a whitewashed building with a large, flat roof and long balconies on its side. It was the police station and it immediately reminded Polly of his interview with Chief Inspector Chan. He wondered if anything had been reported to the dean. Anthony Bridges had said nothing when he saw him hunched over the latest copy of *The Times* in the Senior Common Room. He looked up, gave Polly a nod and then went back to his paper.

Staring down at the flat roof of the building, Polly could see a fair-haired English boy running to-and-fro, flying a bright blue kite high up, almost over the harbour or so it seemed from his viewpoint.

Polly stopped at the rails to see where the kite would go. As he looked up to the sky, he saw that it was full of kites of all shapes and sizes, some in the form of dragonflies, highly gilded; some huge butterflies, with bright marks on their wings, the most sinister in the shape of sharks, with sharp, predatory teeth painted on their edges. These aerial fighters were the pride of their young 'pilots', positioned at strategic points on the roofs of buildings, sometimes balancing precariously on ledges. There were territorial demarcations even in the skies, areas where only the 'dragonflies' could go and others where 'sharks' prevailed. The pilots kept a close look out of the horizon. When alien types intruded, the great sky battles began, epic duels in which the glistening, glass-powdered strings of rivals cut across each other until one of them snapped leaving one kite soaring high in victory, the other floating fatally downwards towards the water.

As he walked along Caine Road, Polly looked down at the ships and sampans and ferries. There was a heat haze hanging over the light green water and in the far distance, above Kowloon, loomed the mysterious Lion Rock and beyond that, not so many miles away, on the other side of the border the Red Army was amassed. How long would the 'Fragrant Harbour' last? No one seemed to be particularly concerned about it or allowed the thought to interfere with their daily rounds. The threat of invasion hung over sun-drenched Hong Kong like a distant, black cloud making the glittering, bright present seem utterly unreal.

Through the greenery and the buildings sloping down towards the Central district, Polly could see Government House, with its whitewashed walls and green, tiled roof and elegant pagoda, towering in the sun. There it nestled, in supreme tranquillity in its own garden, great bronze lions guarding the door. Proud they looked, and fierce, but would they be any more effective against the boots of the Red Army than they had been against the Japanese a decade or so before? And this time, would surrender be decided before a huge loss of life? Even now as Polly gazed down at the building, was the same futile debate taking place within its grand salons—how many men would be sacrificed in defending the indefensible? What price would be demanded by honour?

And after it was all over, how to explain it? Then Polly and his cronies, the historians, like vultures, would move in for the kill, to pick the bones clean, to mull over causes and effects. Was there an exact moment after which the sequence of events that followed became inevitable? Could anything have been done to avoid the final collapse? Who was to blame? Was there a single cause, a person whose actions were decisive, an underlying factor that could not be ignored? And what of his own situation witnessing the collapse of the system? Did that affect the writing of history; was it part of the history or just part of the writing?

Polly was pondering these weighty matters as he entered the gates of the Botanical Gardens, passing its stone lion guardians. His nostrils were assailed by the humid, pungent smell of turned earth, of fresh planting. This was the best time to come to the gardens, in the early evening when everyone bypassed them to rush home to sip a cold beer or play *mahjong* or, if they were lucky, to luxuriate in air-conditioned rooms. In the garden, everything was peaceful: the frail brown sparrows pecked at the dry grass and the bees hummed merrily as Polly walked along inspecting the flower beds, with neat herbaceous borders. Everything was ordered and in its place.

Polly wished that he knew more about tropical plants. The profusely flowering hibiscus, yellow and pink, was easy enough, but what of the star-shaped pink and white flowers, the bush that was like a magnolia, but even more graceful, the petals that closed as soon as you touched them? He had reached the ponds, with their rich water-lilies floating and gaudy goldfish swimming around each other. Around the surface of the water, dragonflies were buzzing. There was a gentle shimmer on the late afternoon water, it was utterly tranquil, only the sound of the city buzzing in the distance.

Polly found a bench with a view down the sloping banks. Through the thick foliage, he could make out the pagoda of Government House jutting up at what seemed an impossibly acute angle. Polly thought to himself: did this stillness accentuate sound? How was it that he could hear everything so precisely, even the thoughts forming in his own mind?

Then he began to think again about that stifling afternoon in Kowloon. He wondered if Chief Inspector Chan would report him to the dean. And if he had, what had they agreed to do about it? The policeman had shown no interest in his moral life, no concern with anything except the practical consequences of his behaviour. It seemed that he would do nothing unless Polly made another move. And was that bound to happen? Was it predetermined, or could he exercise free will even if it involved acting out of character?

And what of his connections with England? Auntie Elsie in the small, cramped house in the suburbs, the grey skies, the grey faces, the never-ending talk of how during the war everything had been so exciting, such a sense of community! Drab years of rationing and making do while he, Polly, lived a life of luxury in Hong Kong, far more luxury, in fact, than he needed for his modest needs.

No doubt that was why Ah Hing had no respect for him. She preferred to work for proper 'foreign devils' like Colonel Hicks, who was full of awkward demands and unreasonable requests. That kind of behaviour was expected of barbarians. With Polly, quiet and undemanding, Ah Hing did not know where she stood, and she did not like it. And then Polly did not keep his proper distance. Why did he spend time talking to Ah Tang, the gardener? He was the master of the house; it would be enough just to give instructions, no need to lose face exchanging pleasantries with someone who was just above the level of a common coolie. If Polly diminished his status by doing such things, it also affected Ah Hing. She lost face because her master was not proud. All the servants on University Drive, the most prestigious address on the campus gossiped about his odd behaviour, really not fitting for a master. It was not dignified to work for someone who was not taken seriously; it didn't matter whether he was liked or not.

Suddenly, Polly was annoyed with himself. How absurd, he thought, being worried about Ah Hing and her views. At any rate, there was no doubt about *her* allegiance; he had never come upon a more transparent card-carrying member. But all these thoughts were a waste of time He should instead be concerning himself with more important matters, how to progress with his universal history, for example.

Polly was aware that someone else had come through the gates of the gardens and was heading towards his bench. He looked up quickly to see a well-dressed Chinese man, probably in his thirties (why was it so difficult to judge the age of the Chinese?), with a sharp, pale face, gold-rimmed glasses and brylcreemed hair exuding its cloying scent. Turning away to avoid his eye, Polly knew that the man had sat down on the same bench, at the other end. But it was too late; the man caught his eye, gave a polite nod and pulling out a gold case from his pocket, offered Polly a cigarette.

"I don't smoke," said Polly, stiffly.

"But there is no smoke without fire," responded the stranger in fluent English, lighting a cigarette for himself.

Polly was taken aback. He took another look at the man. No, he did not recognise him, he could not place him. He was certainly too old to be a student. There were few mature students on campus. Polly would have recognised him if he had been one. Was he perhaps an attendant in one of the science laboratories? It was possible. As Polly knew, nothing could be deduced about people's status from their clothes in Hong Kong. The humblest dressed smartly; sometimes the very rich dressed very simply. Was he a swimming pool guard? The bookshop manager whom he had only seen once or twice? Polly could not place him.

"No, you don't know me," said the stranger, seeming to read his thoughts. "Allow me to introduce myself. I am Simon Wing, please call me Simon."

Polly stiffened. He must be from the police.

"I suppose you know who I am?" He said.

"You are Augustus John Polly, Reader in Comparative History, an expert on the Ottoman sultans."

"You are very well informed, Mr Wing," said Polly curtly, "and may I ask how you know who I am and what you want?"

"Oh, Mr Polly. How long have you been in China? Surely you know that we don't do business like that? We Cantonese don't like to rush into things. Let's not hurry, let's take our time. I've always enjoyed good conversation and it's not every day that one has the chance to talk to someone as distinguished as you."

"Your English is remarkably good," said Polly, returning the compliment.

He knew that this was the start of the game of face-giving which was obligatory if he wanted to find out anything at all. It was a question of flattering the person at the same level as they flattered you. Eventually, when the civilities had escalated to an acceptable level, they could drop all pretence and get to the point. It took time. It required patience. But, in any case, whether he found out anything or not, Polly suddenly felt the desire to beat Simon Wing at his own game, for once to outmanoeuvre an inscrutable Chinaman.

"You must have studied abroad?"

Mr Wing laughed. "Well done, Mr Polly. Cornell, actually. I had a good grounding though, Hong Kong U! But don't worry, it was before your time, Mr Polly, you haven't forgotten someone you should have remembered."

"Well, I'm glad my predecessors did such a good job. And at Cornell, what did you study?"

"History of philosophy," said Mr Wing. "I studied under AJ Lovejoy, a wonderful, wise man. Pity about his politics though."

"But I thought he was one of the great liberal teachers of his time?" Polly said.

"He was," said Mr Wing, "that's what I mean. A woolly liberal though a good man and a great scholar."

There was a pause. A slight breeze rustled the trees and the pagoda of Government House came into view again. Mr Wing motioned towards the tower.

"Ever been in there?" He said and before Polly could reply he continued, "I have a number of times for special meetings with the governor."

Now Polly was curious. Mr Wing was more than just another well-educated police officer who had studied abroad. He gave the impression of being used to high-level dealings, to taking decisions when the time came. His manner exuded confidence.

"Special meetings with the governor," said Polly, "sounds very grand and important."

Mr Wing turned to face Polly directly.

"Grand, yes, Mr Polly, important, I do not think so." He paused for a moment, and then added, "At any rate, not from the historical point of view."

"Well, if you mean *sub specie aeternitatis*, then I suppose nothing is important," Polly replied.

The two men sat in silence for a few minutes. Only the sound of the cicadas could be heard croaking in regular rhythm. The two strangers were sizing each other up like animals in the wild. Mr Wing resumed the conversation as if there had been no pause.

"What interests me greatly, Mr Polly, is this idea of yours about 'ultimate history'. I know that you have been working on this theme for some time."

"How do you know that?" Polly asked more out of a need to collect the full story rather than to quiz Mr Wing about his method of operation which Polly knew, in any case, would be a waste of time.

"It's widely known, Mr Polly. You've lectured on the subject; you've written a piece about it which we all look forward to reading. You even bring it up on launch picnics!"

Polly smiled. "Bringing it up," was not a bad description of what had happened at the Lam launch picnic.

"Since you are so well informed, Mr Wing, I am surprised that you don't know my conclusions."

Now Mr Wing smiled. "But, Mr Polly, that's not fair. You haven't let out the secret yet."

"'Ultimate history' is not going to be available, if I can put it that way—it makes history sound like a product you buy in a department store like Wing On Ltd—until all the facts are known."

He realised how sententious this sounded, but how else could he have put it?

"But in the meantime?" Mr Wing asked, "Surely one has to begin somewhere?"

"Oh, one does," said Polly, in his most donnish mode, "one does by a careful accumulation of facts, facts of course selected for their validity, not just any facts…"

Mr Wing paused momentarily.

"Yes, I understand that, Mr Polly. But once you have collected the relevant facts, once you have analysed them, then you start to develop the theories, don't you?"

"Yes," said Polly, "hypotheses I prefer to call them. At this stage, nothing is finally established and conclusions are still some way off. One has the problem too that history is repeated, over and again. As far as we know the Ottoman Empire doesn't exist anymore, but its history is written and re-written over and again. So, in a certain way it continues to exist, but in many different forms depending on who is describing it."

"But if we have all the right facts," Mr Wing added, "then we can begin the business of 'ultimate history'."

"Yes," said Polly, "but that's the problem, how to know that you have got all the relevant facts? It takes time, years, decades to get anywhere near that point."

"I admire your patience, Mr Polly. We Chinese make a virtue of patience. We believe that with patience, everything is attainable. So even your 'ultimate history' may be attainable."

"How encouraging," Polly laughed, "how encouraging."

"On the other hand," said Mr Wing, "there may be shortcuts. Ways of getting things moving a bit more quickly, and getting out of the fog which we are all walking through. A revolution or two to give us a better idea of how historical laws work?"

Polly waited. He knew what Mr Wing was getting at. This was orthodox stuff. And he let him go on because he had often pondered about the relationship of his 'ultimate history' to Marxism. He acquiesced, intellectually, in the direction Mr Wing was taking because he had not dismissed the possibility of a connection himself.

"You are talking about something else now," Polly said, a trifle too briskly.

"We were talking a short while ago as historians. We were discussing the possibility of deriving a theory of history from a collection of facts. We were looking at a canvas, considering the colours that had been painted onto it. But now you want to be part of the painting yourself. To be an agent in it."

"Oh yes, that is true, Mr Polly, that is true. But aren't you in the canvas too? Even as an historian, aren't you part of the painting that you are looking at, that you are describing? Isn't it possible to be in it as well as to describe it?"

Polly did not answer straight away. He looked closely at Mr Wing whose expression had changed. His good humour and affable manner seem to have disappeared. He looked stern, even gaunt. In the fading light, his eyes shone fanatically.

"And how much of the picture is ready?" Polly said, dropping his voice.

"Oh much, Mr Polly, much. Don't forget that we have had four thousand years of Chinese history. Quite a long time to accumulate facts. Quite long enough for us to predict how things will turn out."

"Reaching the point of 'ultimate history'?" Polly said, hardly believing that he was voicing the words himself.

"Mr Polly, consider what you said before. Ottoman history is your speciality. But you know that the Ottoman Empire is finished: you know that the Sultan-Conqueror is not going to ride into Constantinople again, that Suleiyman the Magnificent is not going to conquer territories again, that the Macrovadotas, the Cantacuzenos, the Koprulus are not going to rise from the dead and begin to stalk the streets of modern Istanbul. It's all there, it's closed. Moreover, all the facts are there: 'ultimate history' is waiting to be written."

"And China?"

"It's the same story, Mr Polly. Our feudal China is over, for good and all. Tang horses and elaborate calligraphy must be weighed against bound feet and peasant starvation. But it can all be collected, all written up because, like your Ottoman Empire, it is all over. Dead and buried. There is no holding on, certainly no going back. It's over."

"And General Chiang Kai Shek?"

"An anachronism," Mr Wing replied, "no more effective than some old Bey left in charge of a distant Ottoman province after the empire had already collapsed at the centre."

Polly looked at Mr Wing again. Could this man be right? Sitting here, in the Botanical Gardens, with Government House in view, could he be right in predicting the end of an empire: British, Chinese, Eurasian; a great cosmopolitan monster, lying at their very feet, breathing its last breath.

"Supposing for a moment you are right," said Polly, "what difference does it make to me? Marxist dogma is too narrow, too unthought out to form the basis of historical reasoning."

"That remains to be seen," said Mr Wing, "but we do need you, Mr Polly. Our faith is narrow, as you say, but it has to be, at first, to keep its purity. Then things change, they evolve. What is important is to be going in the right direction, in the general swim. This is where you can help us. You need to become part of the picture as well as its observer, an historian. But as an historian, it will be left to you to write our 'ultimate history'."

Polly was dazzled. Was it too much exposure to the sun? Too much after the interview with Chief Inspector Chan, too much heady talk with this stranger whose manner and voice were so persuasive, dispelling doubts that Polly had for so long? He felt his head spin, he felt his old vertigo which came at times of tension; he could smell Auntie Elsie's lavender water which was sprinkled on his face when he had fainted as a boy. His vision was fading, everything was becoming a blur.

Then Polly became aware of Mr Wing calling out in a frightened voice.

"Mr Polly, Mr Polly. Are you alright? Can you hear me?"

Mr Wing was leaning over him. Polly could see the blurred outline of his face, but instead of his slanted dark eyes, the deep blue irises of Dean Meissen stared down at him. Instead of jet-black hair, Mr Wing now had the auburn hair of Fiona Meissen and smelt, as she had smelt earlier that day, pungent and sexual. Then Polly noticed that Mr Wing was not wearing his shirt any longer, his exposed chest was bulging and muscular; he had the brown torso of Ah Tang the gardener, the same wispy hair sticking out from his underarms. Polly leaned forward to sniff the scent of caraway seed, but as craned his neck, his vision blurred altogether into a mesh of grey, bluish grey, with horizontal lines flashing across it…

When Polly came to his senses, he had no idea where he was. He became aware of something pressing on his back: it was the wooden ribs of the park seat chaffing his spine. He could hear the birds chirping. As he lifted himself gingerly, he smelled the strong, musky smell of Tiger Balm oil which was close to his nostrils and on his forehead. He recognised Mr Wing staring at him and saw the relief that now showed in the Chinaman's expression. How on earth had Mr Wing managed to get him onto the bench or had he already been on it when he had the blackout?

"Thank goodness for Tiger Balm!" said Mr Wing, "How do you feel now?"

Polly sat up, still resting his head on the bench. He did not know if he would suddenly be hit by another blackout or whether the buzzing in his head, a more familiar and less frightening affliction, would come instead. He felt no pain, but a strange lightness as if he had no weight. His mouth was completely dry, his lips were cracked.

"I'm alright, thank you," he said. Then he felt a surge of recovery, even strength. "And what is more, I have come to a decision."

Polly could see that Mr Wing looked surprised. What a strange man was Augustus John Polly. For all his being a 'foreign devil', Mr Wing could not help feeling a growing liking for him. He sat down on the bench next to Polly.

"Take it easy, Mr Polly and let's see how we can get you home," he said in a gentle tone. "We can discuss all that later. We are not going to disappear, you know. There's time."

Polly pulled himself into a fully upright position. He put his hand on the back of his neck to see if there had been any bump from his fall.

"No, you are wrong," said Polly, feeling a bump on his head, but one which he had always had. "There isn't much time. What's the game plan? There must be one."

At that very moment, there was a loud squawk. It came from a swan, swimming in the pond, whose beak had become entangled in the weeds and who screeched out in anger trying to free itself.

Mr Wing hesitated. For the first time, he felt he had lost the initiative. Looking around to check that they were still alone, he said.

"Very well, but there is no need to go so far today."

Polly waited. The swan had stopped its noise.

"We know about your particular proclivity," said Mr Wing, "or shall we call it a speciality?"

Polly shifted in his seat uncomfortably.

"We know about your interview, let's call it that, with the suave Chief Inspector Chan. Never gets ruffled, does he, even when delivering a caution? Oxford training, I daresay."

Polly had reddened. How could they possibly know? Was this just a bluff to get him to incriminate himself? Was this some trick of the university authorities to find a reason for getting rid of him? Anything was possible in the closed, stifling community of Hong Kong.

"I don't know what you are talking about," said Polly.

"But I am sure you do," Mr Wing countered, in a slightly menacing tone.

"You should rely on facts you know, not rumours," retorted Polly.

"Look," said Mr Wing in a sharper tone, "you just said we haven't time to waste. We have read our H.G. Wells too, we know about Mr Polly and his history."

Polly knew that it was no use pretending. Somehow they did know, somehow they had the information. Had he been followed that afternoon? Had Clarence or Laura suspected something and had him watched all the time he had been with Anthony Bridges? Had someone at the police station passed the information on? The chief inspector himself? The young PC who had brought in the tray? It all seemed so unlikely, but somehow the information had got out. Polly's thoughts turned to conspiracy again. Everyone was part of it—the dean, Bridges, students and of course, the chief inspector.

With a flourish, Mr Wing took out his wallet. Flapping it open, he plucked out a new one-dollar note, crisp and green, from a large bundle. He held it up to the light so that Polly could see it clearly—the great, monumental building of the Hong Kong & Shanghai Bank etched on the note. From his shirt pocket, Mr Wing took out a cigarette lighter. He flicked back its shiny cap, sparked it and in a deft stroke set the dollar bill alight. Polly watched the image of the Hong Kong & Shanghai Bank disappear before his eyes.

Mr Wing blew out the flame before it reached the very edge of the note held between his index finger and thumb. He let the last piece of the note float off to the ground. Charred bits of paper fluttered in the air. Mr Wing stood up, took out a white handkerchief and wiped his hands. He put the handkerchief away and nodded at Polly who was still seated on the bench. Without saying another word, Mr Wing strode down the gravel path at a measured pace…

# Chapter 11

The next day Polly, freshly showered and relaxed, walked on to the veranda of No. 3 University Drive to gaze out onto the lawns, verdant after the rain that had fallen in the night, with colourful orange and yellow herbaceous borders of hibiscus, marigold and pansies. Looking down the hill, his gaze swept past the Old Building towards the harbour, crowded with ships and junks and vessels of every size. He could see the green and white Star Ferries cutting relentless paths through everything that was afloat, majestic in their assurance. In the distance were the purple hills of Kowloon—the nine dragons—and beyond, the vastness of China, with its teeming masses and sun-baked paddy fields.

Polly marvelled at the calm, balsamic atmosphere and the fragrance of the flowers in front of him. He enjoyed the dank air coming up from the ground, the more so because he knew that by late morning, the sun would be beating down remorselessly, desiccating all beneath it. Suddenly he felt a sense of liberation: he had a narrow escape but nothing had been lost. He could carry on as if nothing had happened, although he knew that Chief Inspector Chan now had a file on him and may have reported him to Meissen, even though the dean had given no indication of it.

The prospect of a week without lecturing filled him with a feeling of idleness that was almost sensual. Of course, there were always the unfinished tasks—the half-completed paper on Mehmed II for *Byzantine Studies*, unread undergraduate essays, the newspapers from England, arranged in strict, chronological order—Polly found it amusing to imitate the fastidious district officer in one of Somerset Maugham's short stories who opened his papers on the corresponding days of each month—letters that needed answering, some already months overdue.

But today, thought Polly, is not a day for chores or for work of any serious nature. Let everything be piled up neatly on his desk. That at least gave him the impression that he would be efficient and sort everything out quickly when he had a mind to turn to it.

But now was not the time. Now he was going to cross the harbour to Kowloon to meet Anthony Bridges, Clarence, Laura and Susan Chowder—never the best of friends since the incident over Pierre Bayle's footnotes—for a *dim sum* lunch to mark the Autumn Festival. It would certainly be a noisy affair. The Cantonese were never more jovial than on festive occasions. Elders presided over great gatherings of the family around large, round tables in the restaurant. The youngsters concentrated on stuffing themselves with course after course of delicacies brought round by roving waitresses who would screech out the name of the dish they were carrying. The noise was deafening, but no one seemed to notice.

Polly had always been struck by the contradictions in the Oriental character, at least in the character of the Cantonese. So quiet and calm in the garden, tending to flowers or practising their 'shadow boxing' in silence. Or when they were in class, getting on with their work in neat, subdued rows; they became raucous and noisy in restaurants or at *mahjong* tables. How could it be that these same people, so detached and inscrutable, could enjoy such loud, uproarious meals? No more or less, he supposed, than the normally reticent Englishman at a football match or a demure and stately county gal, mounted and uniformed, braying in pursuit of the inedible across the pleasant green of the English countryside.

Polly's thoughts were interrupted by the chiming of the campus clock. Reluctantly, he got up from his rattan chair, dressed quickly in a blue-striped shirt and baggy white flannels. He wanted to slip out of the house before the arrival of Ah Hing with her nosy look and interfering manner. As he strode out of the university gates, the cream and red No. 3 bus heaved into sight around the corner and obligingly stopped as he flagged it down. As Polly got onto the bus, he was handed a leaflet by a well-dressed man he thought was a fellow passenger. The printed sheet contained a notice in English and Chinese from the Allied Union of Bus Drivers and Conductors.

*Dear Customer: We respectfully suggest that by ending our overtime arrangement for workers unavoidably ill at home or advised not to work by considerations of feng shui, the Company Managers are flagrantly disregarding Article 234 of the Code of Agreement which enshrines this long-standing right. We hope that our ever-esteemed customers will show support by returning this form with a tick in the box at the right-hand corner to any employee of the Company.*

*Signed by the Foremen's Committee*

Polly grinned to himself. What a bizarre arrangement that enabled workers to be paid overtime even if they did not attend work because they objected to the lay out of their free accommodation, for that's what he took the *feng shui* reference to mean.

"It can mean that," Clarence had told him showing him how there was a direct line through which the wind—the *feng*—could sweep through the door of his room and into the quadrangle.

"That would be a very bad location," Clarence continued, "sweeping away all your money and luck. A clear-cut case of bad *feng shui*. Other cases are less clear and then you have to consult the *feng shui* man. He is something between a priest and an exorcist."

"And what does the *feng shui* man do?" Polly said.

"He looks at the living environment, particularly at the direction of the wind. If you are embarking on any major building in Hong Kong, you need to consult the *feng shui* man early on. Otherwise, it can be a disaster."

"What happens if the *feng shui* is not propitious?"

"Well, you may find that people refuse to work in the building or it may need to be re-designed. In the most dramatic case of all a brand-new building had to be pulled down because no one would go into it!"

Polly was amused. How wonderful that in a society as hard-headed about business, superstition still held such sway. It was hilarious that smart company directors, in their flashy western suits and sunglasses, needed to pay attention to the antics of a down-at-heel old *feng shui* man who looked a cross between a tramp and a travelling magician.

"But where does the *feng shui* man gain his knowledge from?" He asked.

"Oh, closely guarded secrets," said Clarence, with a grin. "They use intuition, they study. You know what we Chinese are like, Mr Polly, even students at the Department of History, we are always bent over characters and old script."

Polly smiled at Clarence's undergraduate ebullience. But what a mine of information he was. So smart in his blazer and cravat, so impeccably English in his manner, Clarence had a seemingly inexhaustible stock of stories about Chinese customs, cuisine, medicine and sundry other subjects including, as he now discovered, *feng shui*. Yet Polly always found it hard to fathom what Clarence was thinking. Generations of Lam polish had disguised any show of emotion, though Polly had by now learnt to recognise those tiny signs, a change of tone, a deft evasion of the point, a cough or giggle which might indicate disagreement or embarrassment, even annoyance. It was not that the feelings were not there, they were just very carefully controlled, much hidden from sight.

Polly's bus had now shunted into its parking bay, next to the long, covered arcade that led to the Star Ferry Pier. Before alighting, Polly ticked the box on the Union's form and handed it to the impassive bus conductor. Walking along the pavement, he passed the line of rickshaws which were still in service and would take you anywhere in Central for a few cents. He bought his ferry ticket at the kiosk entrance to the pier and then walked straight ahead onto the gangway which sloped down to the lower deck of the ship.

It was eccentric for a European to travel second class, but Polly did not act out of any democratic scruple. Rather he had decided, as a matter of practicality, that there was no point paying double the fare for the dubious pleasure of clambering up the stairs, in ninety degrees of temperature and more of humidity, to sit on the first-class deck. His fellow passengers on the lower deck, who included tough coolies and large, northern cooks, could not understand what this foreign devil was doing in their midst, but they got out of his way and generally ignored him. Their indifference helped him not to feel completely out of place.

A ferry with its green bottom, white top and star-decorated funnel heaved in, crashing against the wooden pier which shuddered under the impact. A neatly dressed sailor, strategically placed on the pier, snatched the rope that was thrown to him from a colleague on board and lassoed the great iron buoy on the pier with it. In a few minutes, the gangplanks were lowered. The throng of passengers from Kowloon thundered off. The crowd that was waiting to board surged forward. Polly found himself jostled by an old, bronzed coolie dressed in rags, who was carrying two cane baskets, in the traditional way, at each end of a long, bamboo pole. As the mob of people stampeded onto the deck, the ferry tilted to one side. Without losing balance, the sailors on board stoically pulled up the gangway.

Polly had boarded last, but he still found himself a seat, with perforated holes on it in the shape of a star. He took out a book from his jacket pocket and put it on his lap, watching the manoeuvres of the ferry as it was pushed off the jetty and heaved out into the harbour to begin the short crossing. Polly had not hurried, but he felt hot. Even the breeze that came, as the ferry drifted off the pier, was warm. The vessel made its way past moored cargo ships and junks, buffeted by the choppy waves hitting its side. Small sampans and motorised craft criss-crossed in every direction. Polly enjoyed the splashing noise as the boat cut its way through the green water.

He took out the book which he had tucked in his broad jacket pocket. It fell open at the place he had reached.

*In the midst of this immense hall, a vast*
*multitude was incessantly passing; who severally*
*kept their right hands on their hearts; without*
*once regarding anything around them. They had*
*all, the livid paleness of death. Their eyes,*
*deep sunk in their sockets, resembled those*
*phosphoric meteors, that glimmer at night, in*
*places if interment. Some stalked slowly on;*
*absorbed in profound reverie: some shrieking with*
*agony ran furiously about like tigers, wounded*
*with poisoned arrows; while others, grinding*
*their teeth in rage, foamed along more frantic*
*than the wildest maniac. They all avoided each*
*other; and, though surrounded by a multitude that*
*no one could number, each wondered at random,*
*unheedful of the rest, as if alone on a desert*
*where no foot had trodden.*

Not a bad attempt at hell! William Beckford's *Vathek* seemed, at that moment, like a vast parable of the history of the human race, forever condemned to doom and damnation. Any progress that the historian might gleefully trace was followed by decline in what seemed a constant, unchangeable pattern. Circles of destruction, occasional releases from the circles.

Polly had discussed eternal recurrence with Anthony Bridges. His colleague had been at his most sceptical, most like the linguistic philosopher he was, the model of modern, barren rationality.

"I don't know that we can even grasp what we are talking about," he said. "What does the statement 'a constant recurrence of historical events' actually mean? Does it mean that each particle of experience, so to speak, is different from every other? Can each of these particles of experience be measured or recorded in a code like mathematics or music? And what defines such a particle? I just don't know what we are talking about."

Polly could see no point in pursuing the conversation with Anthony Bridges. Instead, he talked about recurrence to Marco Aurelio, the aptly named Brazilian who lectured on the philosophy of history. Marco Aurelio was expansive.

"I think at many levels of explanation, recurrence has significance," he said affirmatively, spreading out his hands, with their delicately tapered fingers in front of him, as he spoke.

"Even within the physics of relativity, one can account for it."

Polly smiled.

"You can, Marco, and no doubt you already have."

Marco Aurelio smiled back, his lively dark eyes narrowing in an almost Oriental appearance. They were sitting in his study, a light airy room at the top of the faculty building. The worst glare of the sun was kept out by the half-drawn blinds, and a huge potted palm gave a refreshing, cool feeling to the room. Marco Aurelio leaned back in his rattan chair and plucked a thin pamphlet from his bookcase.

"Try this, it's a beginning," he said, handing a printed lecture to Polly.

"But you know, we can learn about this experience at other levels. I have had transmissions or flashes of experience from the lives of all kinds of people, such as my great-grandparents."

"Because their lives are still continuing at another level of existence?"

"Yes," he said, "it's like going to see a film, it continues in front of you and you can see it over and over again, but you can't get into it or talk to it or in any way directly experience it. At least we haven't found a way to do that yet."

"Good thing you come from São Paulo, Marco," joked Polly, "if you came from anywhere else in Brazil, I might have said you had been indulging in hallucination, perhaps even in voodoo."

Marco Aurelio laughed. "We Paulistas have our feet on the ground, as you know, Mr Polly."

Polly was still musing on the idea of eternal recurrence and the flames of Eblis when he was jolted as the ferry drifted into the pier at Kowloon with a shudder. He closed his book and jumped up, joining the throng waiting impatiently at the gangway, kept at a yawning angle by the sailor because the ferry was too far away from the pier. The boat was tilted with the weight of the bodies transferred to one side. Suddenly there was a bang as the gangway was lowered and everyone stampeded across the platform and onto the creaking wooden pier. Polly did not rush. Already hot, he did not want to arrive at the restaurant bathed in sweat. Instead, he strolled along the shaded arcades that gave respite from the baking hot streets of Tsim Sha Shui.

When he reached the entrance of the restaurant, he saw himself reflected in the glass door. He had done well not to hurry; he did not look too red or ruffled. As he put his hand towards the huge lion door handle, it moved away, pulled open by a uniformed attendant who bowed as Polly came in. The noise inside was overwhelming. Tables of screaming Cantonese, a people serious in their enjoyment of meals, were crammed together, their clamour added to by the wails of the waitresses who circled with their trays of *dim sum*. In a far corner, Polly spotted Anthony Bridges, standing out a mile in his striped summer blazer and tie, and red English face. How does he do it in the afternoon heat, thought Polly, just as the cold air-conditioning of the restaurant made him shiver.

"Polly, how good to see you," boomed Anthony Bridges, "we haven't started yet, well at any rate, on food," he said with a smirk. "The others are having tea, but its pink gin for me. What will you have, old boy?"

"The old boy will join you in a pink gin," beamed Polly, enlivened by the cool air and determined not to be outdone by Anthony Bridges' suave, oleaginous urbanity.

"How are you, Susan?" He said to Susan Chowder, at the same time nodding at Clarence and Laura who were deep in conversation in Cantonese.

"I'm quite well, Polly," said Susan, "bbbbut I can't fiffinfinfin-ish that chapter," she spat out with effort.

Poor, Susan, thought Polly. Can't get the sentence out because of her wretched stutter, can't finish the chapter because Bayle is quite as contorted a thinker as she is a speaker, a dead end.

"The chapter about disciples of the great man, isn't it?" Polly said and to his relief, Susan just nodded.

"You mean Mandeville and all that Rotterdam crowd," said Anthony Bridges, butting in pompously.

"But Mandeville wasn't an anti-rationalist," chipped in Clarence who had now stopped talking to Laura. "Isn't anti-rationalism your theme, Susan?"

"He was a man of science," Anthony Bridges answered without giving Susan Chowder a chance to come to her own defence. "But in his psychology, he placed a lot of emphasis on the passions. Popularising Hobbes, really."

"Shall we order?" Polly said abruptly, seeing an argument in the making.

"Clarence, what's good here?"

"Yes, let's eat," said Clarence with the enthusiasm of his race for culinary delights. "I'm starving and look at Susan, she's wasting away!"

He glanced down a very long menu.

"How about some delicious octopus, all inky, in ginger sauce with seaweed? Make your teeth go black, but no other known side-effects."

For the rest of the meal, there was no more talk about Bayle or Mandeville or rationalism or anti-rationalism. Instead, they talked about politics. Anthony Bridges was gloomy.

"I reckon its death by a thousand cuts. You'll forgive me saying so," he intoned, waving his chopsticks, still stuck with strips of *chow mein,* in the air, "but you Chinese are masters of the waiting game and of slow torture."

Clarence beamed.

"Oh yes, we are, Dr Bridges. How did you enjoy that last dish, meat in oyster sauce, didn't grandma taste nice?"

Laura frowned. She muttered to Clarence in Cantonese and his smile vanished in an instant. She had decided to launch into an attack.

"As a matter of fact, Dr Bridges, we used to be quite civilised until we came in contact with Westerners, whom you know we call barbarians. The British, actually, haven't a bad record in cruelty," she said. "Have you read how the early riots and uprisings were dealt with in the colony? You should. And what about the other day, in Wanchai? Some quite innocent bystanders beaten up for nothing."

"No race has a monopoly on cruelty," said Polly, trying to calm the atmosphere. "I'm sure Anthony would be the first to agree with that."

Laura did not look mollified but stared at the two dons fiercely.

"Nor does any sex," said Anthony Bridges, deliberately provocative. "But what I meant was that the Chinese will play with Hong Kong like a cat playing with a mouse. They will occasionally scratch us with a claw and then draw back. When it finally suits them, they will just march in. There are thousands of troops not far from the border waiting for their orders."

"According to my parents," said Clarence mischievously, "the Japanese take the cake for cruelty. Shall I tell you what they did in Shanghai after the invasion?"

"No, don't," said Polly firmly, "we have come here to enjoy ourselves, not have an afternoon of horror stories. If I'd wanted that I would have gone to the Roxy cinema for a whole afternoon of Hammer films."

There was a temporary silence. It seemed that each member of the group was wondering what to talk about next. But Polly had succeeded in getting them off the subject of cruelty, Oriental or occidental.

"Tell me something else," demanded Anthony Bridges, sinking back in his seat with a self-satisfied look on his face. "Why do Chinese meals end with soup while ours begin with it?"

"Depends on the kind of meal," said Clarence quickly. "Meals like this are gourmet style. We say that soup dulls the palate for the fine dishes to follow. But in ordinary meals, you can have the soup at the same time. Slurp it up together with the noodles if it's *wun tun* or something like that. In those kinds of meals, family meals if you like, the order of the dishes doesn't matter at all. You eat whatever comes along first."

Polly was not listening. His thoughts had started wandering, particularly as a faint buzz began in his ears as Clarence was speaking. He found the air-conditioning, which was all the rage in smart restaurants, too cold. Suddenly he was reminded of Chief Inspector Chan's office. To his relief, the buzzing did not increase in volume, and he knew that he was not about to suffer anything serious. It would subside in a moment. As he looked across the table, he saw Laura staring at him, a hard stare, like an examiner who was assessing him for a purpose he didn't fully understand. When she saw that he was looking at her, she began speaking.

"I see that you are reading William Beckford's *Vathek.* Are you enjoying it?"

"It's an outrageously overdone tale," said Polly, "quite amusing in parts; the decor and costumes are worthy of a Hollywood movie."

"And what about the character of the Caliph," she added, "do you find Caliph Vathek a sympathetic hero?"

"He has his good points," said Polly, "but he has his weaknesses too. There is a self-destructive element there."

"The fatal flaw, again?" Clarence said, getting up. "Was he arrogant, like Wilde's Dorian Gray?" He said as he got up and walked towards the cashier's desk.

"I don't know if Dorian Gray was exactly arrogant," said Polly.

"He didn't doubt his own worth, though," sneered Anthony Bridges, "though I grant you that that's not the same as being arrogant."

"Vathek's arrogance," said Polly, ignoring his colleague's intervention, "consisted in a belief that he was omniscient. His deep curiosity, something which hardly seems a vice to people like us, was linked to a mad desire to dominate fate, to control his own destiny. That goes against Koranic teaching and it led to his downfall."

"Or," said Laura straightaway, "was it the flames of Eblis that he could not resist? The crackling, burning flames?"

Polly did not like the insinuating tone in her voice. Before he could think of a riposte, Clarence had reappeared.

"Well, let's go," he announced, confirming with those innocuous words that he had already paid the bill, out of sight, Hong-Kong style. Anthony Bridges and Polly both stood up at the same time. They had been in the Far East long enough to know that it would be the height of bad manners to offer their share of the bill or even refer to the fact that it had been paid at all. Clarence, although only a student was the host, it was up to him to deal with such matters. It was as simple and as subtle as that.

Two o'clock struck and the restaurant had all but emptied. The tables were laden with used dishes and chopsticks, countless platters and plates, hundreds of teapots and thousands of bowls to be collected, emptied, cleaned, and restored. Polly was always reminded of a battlefield scene in any Chinese restaurant, especially at the end of a banquet. But Clarence told him that debris was essential. Otherwise, no one could be sure that the meal had been enjoyed.

Even though the mess this time is gargantuan, it is impressive thought Polly to himself.

When they stepped out of the large, frosted-glass doors onto the pavement, the afternoon heat hit their air-conditioned bodies with a vengeance. Sometimes the heat seemed like a vicious demon intent on damaging you, breathing heavily on you, determined to make you as uncomfortable as possible. Polly shivered as his body tried to adjust to the violent contrast of temperature.

"I do find that the air conditioning affects you badly," he said.

"You mean its absence hits you," said Anthony Bridges, pedantically, "but isn't that the case with most good things in life?"

Clarence grinned. He and Laura had hailed a taxi and with a cheerful wave, jumped into it and disappeared.

"I'm offff to to to Kelly and WWWWalsh…" said Susan Chowder, slurring badly.

Neither Polly nor Anthony Bridges tried to dissuade her. They watched as Susan's lonely figure, clutching a briefcase full of papers and books, made her way off towards Nathan Road.

"Poor thing," said Anthony Bridges, clutching his brolly at the door of the restaurant, "what a way to go through life."

# Chapter 12

"I want to stress," intoned Polly, "the cosmopolitanism of the Ottoman empire which, contrary to our European view of it"—Polly realised the inappropriateness of the phrase as soon as he had used it—"was to a large extent open and tolerant in a way not matched in historically contemporary Western countries. Greeks, Jews, Armenians, Europeans and Arabs lived together in perfect accord under Ottoman rule. Members of these foreign communities achieved high office in the service of the sultans. The business of the empire was conducted in many languages, with records kept in Greek-by-Greek officials. The sultans themselves were often cultivated men who might speak an array of languages and be familiar with the literature of several cultures. They did not view the mixed, multi-racial element of the society they ruled over as in any way a disadvantage. In that sense, the Ottoman Empire was a true successor to Constantinople and, in its turn, to Rome. The Roman principle that citizenship existed wherever the empire spread—*civis Romanus sum*—had its successor. The Ottoman equivalent was in the belief that one culture is not sufficient for an intellect."

Polly paused for a moment and looked around the lecture hall. It was another humid day; the ceiling fans whirred and through the open window he could see the sprinkler on the lawn keeping the dean's grass green and Ah Tang's neatly kept borders.

"Any questions?" He asked, hoping there would be none. But Laura Li had raised her hand.

"Yes, Laura, some constructive comment, I am sure?" He asked as the rest of the class tittered.

"I wanted to ask about this particular matter of the races mixing," said the unstoppable Laura. "I thought you told us before that the different communities living in Constantinople wore different clothes, hats, and coats for example, and that they were obliged to do so. Well, how does that tie up with the so-called cosmopolitanism you are emphasising now?"

Polly smiled genially. Trust Laura to pick that up, he thought to himself. She was as sharp as ever.

"Living in a cosmopolitan society doesn't mean that people don't have any roots," he answered smoothly. "It's a matter of living in a society where a mix of cultures is taken for granted, each person living in his own way but understanding that others will live in theirs. It's not a question of having to give up your taste or identity; it's a matter of tolerating and enjoying a mix."

"Don't have to rule out bangers and mash just because you eat chow mein," chipped in Clarence, who was sitting next to Laura, dressed in his usual immaculate attire of dark blazer and crisp white shirt.

"Yes, that sort of thing," said Polly, "communities may co-exist and enjoy the differences in their respective dress, food and religion."

"And would you say that was the case in the British empire?" Laura said provocatively.

"Up to a point," said Polly. "I don't think there has been any systematic attempt to suppress indigenous culture, even customs and laws. For example, in Hong Kong, as you know, Chinese practices are taken into account in applying English law, especially in settling disputes in rural areas. But I think that true cosmopolitanism is easiest in a city, a smaller area with a distinct sense of place. That was certainly the case for Constantinople and indeed for Rome."

"But Hong Kong is a city," persisted Laura, "and I hardly think going on a picnic in a Lam launch qualifies for a mix of cultures, does it, Mr Polly?"

Clarence grinned at the reference to his family's well-known way of entertaining 'foreign devils'.

"Never just provide Cantonese food," his grandfather used to say, "The devils, being more combustible, need their own kind of fuel. Especially a supply of San Mig."

"No," said. Polly reasonably, determined not to be ruffled, "that, in itself, would not be enough. One would need to be a little more committed, or as the French say *engagé*, with Chinese culture, with Chinese people, for cosmopolitan to be a just description."

"But that's the trouble," said Clarence. "We Chinese don't actually like foreigners much. We are only interested in our own ways; we certainly don't want to adopt yours. So, who is more of the imperialist?"

"If you're talking about mainland China," said Polly, "the situation is complicated by the fact that communism is in any case not an indigenous product. It is an importation, a foreign system brought into China."

"But it has been adapted to the needs of the Chinese people," said Laura in a hostile tone, "and to that extent it is a bulwark against foreign imperialism."

Polly was about to qualify her remark, then thought better of it.

"I think we are getting a bit far away from the Ottomans. But, in any case, I was coming to an end. Let me finish off with a paradox for you to mull over before the next class. The cosmopolitanism which survived in the Ottoman Empire until the early nineteenth century was eventually compromised by a rampant nationalism that came from the West, but which affected the local communities in the capital, Constantinople. That led to serious unrest. In 1819, there was a Greek uprising which was severely dealt with by the Sultan. Then there was trouble in the Balkan provinces. You know about Mr Gladstone and his speech in the House of Commons on the Bulgarian massacres. The local military commander had taken stern, savage action in the face of local disturbance which led to a backlash. But let us return to the centre of what, after all, was a centralised system of administration. I want to end by linking the fate of the Ottoman Empire, the reason for its decline, to the very source of its previous, enduring vitality. That source was the absolute nature of the Sultan's governance. When that power had been used wisely, with tolerance and magnanimity, it was strength. If you like, it was the glue that kept the whole collage together. But when it became the implement of suppression, when it started to be used to stamp out the local sentiment, it became a weakness, an Achilles heel through which the whole body politic would be attacked. That change in the exercise of despotic power is the crucial factor in the decline of an empire that had survived, on the whole successfully, for almost five hundred years."

Polly stopped, abruptly closed his file and left the rostrum without giving Laura Li a chance to prolong the argument about China and the West. Walking out of the lecture hall, he crossed the shaded courtyard, along the dark, tiled corridor reaching the path that led back towards his house, sweating under the weight of his black gown. When he entered the hall of No.3 University Drive, he flung his gown onto the wide-armed chair. He was soaked in sweat. He went straight upstairs to the bathroom and throwing all his clothes in a heap on the floor, stood under the shower allowing himself a drenching for five gloriously long minutes.

Polly knew that this was highly unsociable behaviour at a time when there was a severe water restriction in the colony. On the other hand, he asked himself, how many people in Hong Kong are forced to wear a heavy black gown to work every day? And how many others have to argue the causes of the decline of empires with difficult Laura Lis? Polly smirked at the thought of Alistair Crowley's expression as if he had heard the discussion about the end of the empire. He certainly would not have approved but how could he have convinced anyone that, uniquely, the British Empire would endure forever?

"I tell you the man is a Red," Crowley would state as he heard Polly explaining that the Ottoman empire had collapsed because of authoritarian suppression of minorities. For what else was the governance of their own colony cloaked in? How else could a paltry ten or twenty thousand white men control a vast mass of Chinese? If authority was challenged, the bluff would be called and all would be lost. So, no one was permitted to rock the boat, in however small a way. That was the official line and anyone who dared to challenge it would be in trouble. One only had to look at what was happening in Malaya to see the results of laxity, of too much freedom.

Polly stepped out of the shower and stood naked, staring at his body in the long mirror fixed on the bathroom door. Not a wonderful figure, but at least not bloated. He began to dry himself with a large, white towel. He thought again about his lecture: well, he could do nothing against the paranoia of the authorities. After all, his job was to present history; to look at causes and effects in the past, not to predict what was going to happen either in Hong Kong or anywhere else. If others drew conclusions from his work, there was nothing he could do about that.

Polly wrapped the towel around his waist and, still dripping, made his way across the landing to his study. The room was dark, the shutters down to keep out the heat of the day. His desk was covered in papers, in various piles, which waited for attention. One pile was made up of official letters and bills, the sort of correspondence he most detested and which he only answered when it could be left no longer. Another pile consisted of personal letters, topped by an envelope posted in Beckenham with a stamp of the new, young Queen on it. It was from his aunt Elsie who had just seen the coronation. Polly took the letter out of its Basildon Bond envelope, unfolded it and read.

*We were in Trafalgar Square, absolutely packed,*
*when the coaches came along the Mall, all*
*aflutter with children waving Union Jacks. The*
*young Queen looked so radiant, so serious.*
*Afterwards we went to Lyons Corner House to*
*celebrate with a cup of tea.*

Polly could imagine the scene. Elsie was up from Kent for the day, with a hat and matching handbag, probably only a few shillings in her purse and a sturdy umbrella too, because you never knew. Even now in her seventies, Aunt Elsie was trim and neat, exuding an air of reliability with her square handbag and sensible shoes. He remembered making that trip with her as a boy, feeding the pigeons in Trafalgar Square and then the mounting excitement as they made their way along the Strand towards the glistening window of Stanley Gibbons. Seeing all the rows of neat stamps in the glass cases. Kings' and queens' heads, with remote and exotic backgrounds, an Indian tiger, a tortoise from the West Indies, some square, colonial building in Malaya. Where was this place (what a lovely purple colour) who was this king with his fluffy beard and hypnotic stare? Why was this only a penny and this five when they looked exactly the same? And afterwards the tea, always in the Lyons Corner House, and, if he was lucky, a sticky bun with a dab of butter, still being rationed.

Polly put the letter down. England seemed far away, and it was not the afternoon to answer letters like Aunt Elsie's. He picked up the heavy, Chinese lion paperweight holding down the pile of bills. On top was the small account book from Ah Chueng, the comprador, with its long lines of items and sums of cost on the side column, neatly ruled by a red margin. Every week Polly would ring up Ah Chueng, telling him the items of food and household goods that he needed. Later in the day the order would be brought around by a panting errand boy, together with the account book, totalled and up to date.

Polly opened the account book again and saw that his bill was overdue. Quite a few weeks overdue. He had better go to Ah Chueng's and settle it.

He got up, still holding the Chinese lion which he now placed on the study mantelpiece. He walked out of the room, across the gloomy hall landing to his bedroom, with its light, bamboo furniture. Opening the wardrobe, he saw a neat row of short-sleeved shirts, starched and perfectly ironed by Ah Hing. Even a Communist sympathiser knows how to iron shirts, he thought to himself, reaching for his lightest, white cotton. Surely, the art of Chinese laundering would continue even under Chairman Mao.

# Chapter 13

Polly strolled down the path towards the university gates where he would catch a bus along Bonham Road in the direction of Upper Levels. As he reached the entrance, he heard his name being called out.

"Polly, Polly, how are you today?"

Polly turned around to see Fiona Meissen in a pretty summer dress and white hat waving at him. She looked at the picture of health and fragrance. Polly crossed over to where she stood.

"Hello, Fiona," he said shyly as he always did when speaking to women unless, for a reason he had never understood, they were Chinese.

"I'm very well, much recovered from the other day on the launch. Sorry to have caused such a commotion."

"Oh, you didn't cause any commotion at all," said Fiona graciously. "George"—how odd to hear the dean called by his first name—"was concerned. In fact, we all were because it can be nasty to get sunstroke, even a touch. That's why I wear this," she said pointing at her wide-brimmed straw hat with a flourish.

"Very sensible of you," said Polly, "I always leave my hat at home and then regret it."

"One can regret too much in life," said Fiona, with sudden feeling, "but what about having tea with me or a drink, if you prefer?"

"Delighted, Fiona. I was on my way to Ah Chueng's to pay my bill, but I don't suppose you want to go somewhere as ordinary as that?"

"Oh, that will do nicely," said Fiona breezily. "There are some tables at the back, let's get them to bring us tea in the garden, under that great tree the Chinese say is so old. That will be divine."

Polly admired Fiona's confidence. But then being the dean's wife, in Hong Kong, you were used to getting things your own way. Yet at that moment, it wasn't Fiona's natural authority that was most on Mr Polly's mind. It was her youthfulness, her *joie de vivre*, such a contrast to the dean's heavy manner.

Admittedly, she was much younger than Meissen, probably about thirty-five as against his fifty-something. Even so, she was remarkable, so crisp, so elegant, so English in the best summer-frock way.

Polly hailed a taxi, knowing that Fiona was not the sort to ramble along in the afternoon heat. Hardly had they got going, with a delicious breeze coming into the windows, when they rounded the corner at Upper Levels and arrived outside Ah Chueng's. The owner himself rushed out of the shop to greet his important guests.

"Mr Polly, how nice of you to visit us," he said in perfect English, "and Mrs Meissen too. We are most honoured by your presence."

"Thank you, Ah Chueng," said Fiona. "I think Mr Polly has some business to do with you and I would rather like some tea. In the garden, if you please."

"Of course, Mrs Meissen, with the greatest pleasure. Won't you wait here a moment while I get someone to put out a proper table for you in the back? Will be done in a moment."

He turned and muttered in Cantonese to a youth seated at the back of the shop who started up and disappeared out towards the garden without a word. Polly went up to the counter, gleaming so spotlessly so that the 'foreign devils'—Ah Chueng's customers—would feel comfortable. Ah Chueng produced his neatly kept account book, with each item ordered and its price in the margin. Polly leaned onto the polished counter and wrote out a cheque for the outstanding amount. Then he took out a few crumpled dollar bills from his pocket.

"Here you are, Ah Chueng, please give this to the delivery boy," he said stuffing the whole bundle into the Chinaman's hands.

Meanwhile, Fiona stood to one side, fanning herself.

"And how is your father, Ah Chueng? How is the general?" she said.

"He is very well, Mrs Meissen. We Chuengs are all gathering soon to celebrate his eightieth birthday. I will hire the whole of the Mai Ling Restaurant and I wonder if you and the dean—and of course, Mr Polly," he added quickly, "would honour us with your presence?"

"Let us know the date," said Fiona, a touch imperiously, "as you know, the problem is always with the dean. His diary is so packed. But thank you all the same. We will try. And now…"

Seeing that the thin, sullen-looking boy had returned, Fiona guessed that things had been made ready. Without another word, she strode out of the back of the shop into the garden. Polly wondered if she knew anything about his interview at the police station.

A table had been dragged into place under the tree, in the shade, as Ah Chueng had instructed. Though it was a simple fold-up type, it had been covered by a delicate Chinese table-cloth and places had been laid out for two. Fiona went over to the table and sat on one of the cushioned chairs. She looked about wondering why Chinese gardens were always such a mess. No idea of symmetry she thought to herself. Some nice features look at the glorious jasmine in its huge round, monochrome, yellow garden pot, or the frangipani to the other side. But no shape, no order, all in a jumble. As Fiona was thinking this, Polly emerged from the dark interior of the shop blinking and shielding his eyes from the harsh glare.

"Come over here, Polly, it's quite cool under the tree. Why do you think Chinese gardens are such a mess?" She asked. "No recognisable borders, all a jumble."

"Well, of course, that's how it seems to us," said Polly, feeling that he was being too rational for Fiona's taste. "But there is a kind of method in it. They believe that anyone can plant trees in a straight line."

Polly remembered his conversation with Ah Tang, the gardener.

"But the random planting we see which seems like a jumble in our eyes, shows that it is the work of a man, not of a child," he continued without a great deal of confidence.

Fiona looked about her with a quizzical expression.

"I can't see any *man's* work," she said, stressing the word in an exaggerated way, "can you, Polly?"

Polly, now sitting next to Fiona, surveyed the garden. It did look like an untidy mess.

"Well, I must admit in this garden…"

He stopped mid-sentence as a servant, in the traditional white tunic, had appeared carrying a tray.

"In this garden what?" Fiona demanded, irritated by Polly's un-colonial way of stopping what he was saying just because a servant, who was, in any case, unlikely to understand English, had appeared and might be offended by his remarks.

"In this garden, I can't see any method either," he beamed, "ah look, tea is ready."

"Wait till it brews," said Fiona. "But look, Polly, it's the same with their music. Awful jangle, really. No harmony, no melody. And then, in the middle of a performance, if you please, someone walks on the stage and starts banging a nail in the wall. It happened the other day at the opera."

Polly grinned. He particularly enjoyed such eccentricities of Chinese theatre. Someone coming on to finish off the set was alien to the Western way of thinking, but in China, it didn't seem to matter.

"It is rather distracting, Fiona," he said in a mischievous tone, "if, of course, you understand the Chinese libretto and enjoy the inharmonious jangle of the instruments."

Fiona smiled in acknowledgement that she had got herself into a trap.

"Tea, Polly?" She said beginning to pour before he could answer. "Help yourself to sugar and milk."

Polly did as he was told. He felt an inward calm, even a kind of joy. The nice thing about Fiona Meissen was that she knew when to stop. How unlike her husband, the dean, who never did, who always spoilt a good story by over-telling it. Was it that Fiona was more subtle than he or was she just better mannered, or, in that quaint phrase of Auntie Elsie, better brought up? For all the academic distinctions that had been showered on the dean, Polly reckoned that his elegant wife was more than his equal in grey matter.

"Polly," said Fiona in a different tone, "you've been married, haven't you?"

Polly flushed bright red. He paused for a moment, before stuttering a reply.

"Ye-Yes, I have been. Briefly when I was young."

"I thought so," said Fiona, "and did you leave your wife, or did she leave you?"

"She left me," said Polly quickly in a hollow voice, surprised at feeling a sudden pang as he thought about what had happened so long ago.

"Because of?"

This was getting rather personal, thought Polly. On the other hand, he felt no hostility in Fiona's probing. In fact, he found her manner gentle and soothing.

"Oh, the usual," he said, "infidelities or alleged infidelities."

Fiona remained silent for a moment. Reaching for her square white handbag, she opened it—the buckle made a loud click in the silence—and taking out a silver box, helped herself to a cigarette. Polly looked around nervously for matches, but Fiona had already lit her cigarette with a lighter she placed on the table. She drew in deeply before continuing.

"Tell me, Polly, do you think that there are sufficient grounds for infidelity when one realises that one is no longer married to the same person? I mean that when the person one is married to is so changed that they are no longer the same person?"

Polly was startled by her question. He hardly dared to draw out its implication. He replied somewhat precisely.

"That would not be a legal ground for separation, would it?"

"No, of course not," said Fiona, "but do you think it is a moral ground for one to act? Would it be morally right to be unfaithful in such circumstances?"

"I don't know about morally right," he answered, "but if it were the case that someone found his or her partner different, radically and unacceptably different from the person that they had first married, then I think they would become unfaithful as a matter of course."

Fiona nodded. She drew on her cigarette again, careful to blow the smoke into the air, away from Polly.

"That's what I thought. After all, it's what happens that counts; we look for the reasons afterwards. Or at least your lot do, historians, I mean. The rest of us just get on with life."

Polly laughed.

"That makes history sound very much like bunk."

Fiona Meissen was no longer listening, as Polly could see. There was a well of tears in her eyes as she gazed into the distance and Polly, thinking of his brief five months' marriage to Maud, felt downcast himself. They finished their tea in silence and when they stood at the front door of Ah Chueng's Fiona bade Polly a brief farewell as she jumped into a taxi and sped off towards Central.

Ah Chueng hovered nervously in the background.

"Was everything ok with the tea?" He asked, sensing that something odd had happened.

"Oh perfect, Ah Chueng, perfectly delicious," said Polly with deliberate breeziness. "I will see you again next month."

"Goodbye, Mr Polly. I will send you a word about the banquet for my father."

"Yes, of course," said Polly who had decided to stroll towards the Upper Levels at a gentle pace. "I look forward to it."

# Chapter 14

Even though it was late in the year, it remained hot and humid. It seemed that an eternity of scorching weeks lay ahead which would only be made bearable by gallons of ice-cold San Miguel for Polly, and an orchard of lime trees and a vat of gin for Anthony Bridges.

Polly had been seeing a lot of Anthony Bridges. As the weeks of term flew by, they began to realise, with some trepidation, that the international seminar, the first of its sort to be organised jointly by the History and Philosophy Departments, was looming uncomfortably close.

"This is really no joke," wheezed Anthony Bridges, sifting through a pile of papers on his desk. "Vico, Talleyrand, Croce and Durkheim and all at ninety-eight degrees Fahrenheit and God knows what humidity."

The sweat was pouring off his considerable bulk as he got up from his desk with one sheet of paper in his hands, waving it in the air.

"And here's Korma, on Sufism in the Oriental Tale, where in the blazes are we going to fit that in, Polly? He's quite mad."

"Professor Korma is from your *alma mater*," said Polly dryly, "he is quite mad, but it's an Oxonian madness that you should be able to deal with. I leave him to you."

Anthony Bridges looked exasperated and Polly's coolness did not relieve him.

"But look, Polly, there isn't a sensible place to put him in. We're not dealing with mysticism, grand metaphysics and all that nonsense, Oxonian or non-Oxonian."

"That may be so," said Polly, "but have you forgotten that Korma is a close friend of the dean? If we are not careful, we will have a furious row with Meissen on our hands."

"Yes," said Anthony Bridges in a tired voice, "you're right, Polly, a special case, *ad hominem*. But still, where the devil shall we fit him in? It's meant to be a seminar on rationalism in history, not on the way of the Upanishads."

"Sufism," said Polly, "but look, put him at the end of the second afternoon. You've got some anti-historicist stuff, pretend he fits in there. Everyone will be exhausted by then, so they won't be listening to him anyway."

Anthony Bridges went back to his desk. Picking up his blue pencil, he ringed the name 'Korma' and with a quick swing of the hand moved him up to the end of the second afternoon, after Susan Chowder on anti-rationalism in seventeenth-century French intellectual history.

"Excellent idea, Polly. I say you are rather good at this sort of thing. Thought of joining the Colonial Office to sort out the garden party invitations?"

They both laughed.

The Garden Party had been an unmitigated disaster. The main problem, as usual, had been separating the few Chinese dignitaries who had been invited from the old brigade of the British Club who heartily disapproved of any 'natives' attending what they regarded as *their* event. To the consternation of Government House, both groups arrived almost at the same moment and had to wait uneasily in line while he and Lady Fogerty tried to greet each guest with the minimum few words that etiquette, as much as good manners, dictated. It had not been a smooth or successful occasion nor did the governor spare Alistair Crowley, whose duties included ceremonial, from blame.

"I hope," said Sir Reginald, in an ominous tone, "that by next month when we have the ministerial visit, things will run more smoothly."

Polly felt some sympathy for the unfortunate Crowley. After all, what could he have done when all the guests arrived at the same time? Change the layout of the hall? Provide two entrances when there was only one?

Crowley, of course, had blamed the Chinese for what had happened. It was those mutton-headed Shantung chauffeurs—the Chinese Geordies as he thought of them—who brought everyone in at the same time. It would never have happened with the sleek Cantonese, he had to admit, who could be relied upon somehow to fix things up and avoid embarrassment. Next time there would be no Northerners, none of those Shantung blockheads, however reliable and loyal they might be, in charge of arrivals.

That was a month ago. Now the colony was still sweltering under blazing suns. When Polly walked out onto his balcony at six o'clock in the morning, he could already feel that it would be a scorching day. Just before participants for the seminar were due to arrive, students had been displaced from the Halls of Residence and told to go home for a week. Lucky, thought Polly, to be in Hong Kong where most of them lived a stone's throw away or could find a bed with relatives, ubiquitous in Cantonese family life. It would be a different story back at home in England. And the students would just disappear quietly off the campus and there wouldn't be any complaints either.

But that was only the beginning. Detailed plans had to be made, practical matters which neither of the dons was good at, needed sorting out; duties had to be allocated between members of staff and suitable students. Polly and Anthony Bridges took only a moment to decide that Clarence Lam had to be in charge at the welcoming desk at Kai Tak Airport. With his suave manners and natural bonhomie, he was the ideal person to deal with nervous professors and sullen Readers arriving from different parts of the world, tired and irritable after long, bumpy flights.

Professor Korma was among the early arrivals. Marching through the noisy, echoing Arrivals Hall, he found his way straight to Clarence's neatly signposted desk.

"Good morning, Professor Korma," said Clarence smoothly. "Welcome to Hong Kong. May I ask you to sign here and then take this small folder in which you will find all the practical information that you will need over the coming week?"

"What a pleasure to hear the mother tongue spoken so well," boomed Professor Korma, his glasses slipping down his nose. "I spent the last ten hours sitting next to some sullen Koreans. Not a word from them! Never mind, I got on with studying the Sufist symbols in William Beckford's *Vathek*."

"What a profitable journey you've had in that case," said Clarence with only the slightest trace of irony in his voice. "But how much of a true Orientalist was Beckford?"

"Oh, very much one," said Korma, then looking round to see if he might be overheard, he said in a quieter voice, "Have you read his *Episodes?* No? Well, you should. Forbidden subjects."

"Perhaps those are the 'missing' stories that Mr Polly, our Reader in History, has been talking about. He has recently been reading *Vathek*."

"Undoubtedly, they are," said Professor Korma, "did you know that Lord (he intoned the 'o') Byron always wanted to read them but that Beckford (the 'o' rounded again) wouldn't allow him to?"

"Because?" Clarence asked, as he was expected to do.

"Because of *Childe Harold*. Not nice. Not nice at all. Byron describes Beckford's house in Sintra as a ruin, with portals gaping wide."

Korma shrugged his shoulders and said no more.

Clarence wondered whether it had been the thought of Byron's remarks or the air conditioning that had made Korma suddenly shiver. Considering the length of the journey he had just completed, he seemed in bubbling form.

"How fascinating, Professor Korma," he said politely. "And now may I now tell you about some of the practical arrangements?"

He produced a map of the island with an inset of the university campus.

"I don't know if you have been here before; this is Hong Kong Island and here is our university pointing to the map. You can see the Old Building near the entrance."

Professor Korma peered myopically at the sheet put in front of him, but he did seem to be listening.

"And you will be staying just here," said Clarence, marking the spot. "If you wait in here a moment or two—its cooler in here than outside—a bus will take you and the Scottish Enlightenment group over on the vehicular ferry."

Professor Korma made no reply. He did not seem keen on sharing his transport with Scottish Enlightenment types, probably all free-thinkers. Much too rational.

"That prig, Adam Smith," he said aloud, earning a nasty glare from Professor Misho Takanowa, the eminent Smith scholar who was patiently waiting at the side of Clarence's desk, "sententious and banal at the same time. Quite an achievement, really."

Suddenly, the door at the end of the hall was flung open and a familiar voice boomed out.

"So, you're here, Korma," shouted the dean, "thought I'd come to meet you myself."

"George," said Professor Korma, "how nice to see you. How is Fiona? Are you looking after that lovely lady well?"

Dean Meissen beamed in a falsely jovial way. He had never liked the easy rapport between Professor Korma and his wife. Not professional, not at all professional.

"Fiona is flourishing," he said with a forced smile, "but how are you, all the way from California? You must be exhausted. Good flight?"

"Not memorable," said Professor Korma, nodding towards Clarence, "air travel is an efficient but demystifying experience."

"Quite agree, old boy," said Meissen affably. "Come on, you are coming in my car, Clarence will sort out the luggage later, no need to worry about that."

The two old college friends—in fact, as undergraduates, they had been the bitterest rivals for every prize and distinction, struggling to outwit each other at every turn—moved off, brushing past Professor Takanowa, who bowed at once, but to whom the dean gave only the curtest nod.

It would be better, thought Clarence, taking in the professor's bow, if he gave up his Japanese mannerisms while staying in Hong Kong. Far better to pretend to come from an obscure province of China whose dialect no one would comprehend than to be associated with a much-hated occupier of not so long ago. Nevertheless, Clarence behaved with impeccable politeness towards the visitor, helping him to understand the map which he had been studying intently.

"Please sign yourself in," said Clarence, handing the professor his own Parker 51 pen and pointing to his typed name on the list. "It's just for us to know you are here. The others are just outside and you will all be driven off in a few minutes."

The professor signed his name, bowed again and stood to one side, looking agitated and fumbling with his collar.

By six o'clock in the evening, all the delegates had arrived. Miriam Allsorts, Reader in Comparative Literature at Berkeley was the last. She had come despite the fact that she had vowed never to attend another conference at which Professor Korma was present. Miriam Allsorts was a large, buxom blonde lady, panting as she came across the tarmac, improbably clutching, next to her briefcase, a badminton racket. Her cheeks were rouged and a deep red lipstick, thicker than any Wanchai lady's, was slapped on her lips.

"Thank you," she wheezed to Clarence. "Has Korma arrived?" She asked sharply.

"Yes, Professor Korma has arrived," said Clarence, "and he has gone off with Dean Meissen. As you know, they are old chums from Oxford days."

"I doubt if Korma is anyone's old chum, as you put it," she snorted. "What decent person could be a chum of that devious, obstreperous plagiarist?"

Clarence was uncertain how to respond but there was no need to since Miriam Allsorts was now on to one of her favourite topics.

"Tried to steal my ideas on Coleridge and the German Aufklärung," she said, academic indignation rising at the recollection, "but I was tipped off. Someone at the university press warned me. I threatened him with an action, and he backed off and withdrew his article, which, I might say, was already at the proof stage by then."

Clarence smiled awkwardly. He was trying to place Miriam Allsort's accent. Something rumbled underneath her clipped New England tones, something distinctly foreign. He remembered Anthony Bridges saying something to Polly about an 'unspeakable member of that unmentionable race'.

And they said the Chinese were racists, Clarence thought to himself, watching Mirriam Allsorts signing herself in with a florid gesture. But why were academics such a neurotic, hypersensitive lot, forever concerned that someone was stealing a march on them when usually they were working on subjects so obscure that it wouldn't make any difference in any case? And what of the much-vaunted ideal of learning for its own sake?

Even so, and contrary to, the gloomy predictions of some faculty members, the seminar ran smoothly. Professor Korma had neatly shunted up a side-track, Professor Takanowa delivered a lecture in such bad English that it was incomprehensible, while Miriam Allsorts, fiercely independent of the whole group, gave what Anthony Bridges said was the best reading he had ever heard of Coleridge's *Kubla Khan* although Polly, who was, after all, the Orientalist, had his reservations. Four days of papers, answers and analysis, the chattering of voices rising and falling in crescendos, rivalling the background sounds of the city. And all the while, the stifling heat around, pouring in through the open windows, making a mockery of the whirring ceiling fan on full blast to cool the gregarious seminarians.

During the dean's summing up, Polly had to rush out of the Great Hall to stop the assiduous Ah Tang from mowing the lawn (wasn't the grass already razor short?) with a petrol mower that roared its efficiency all over the campus. Polly tried to perform his task delicately, unable to be harsh with the virile Ah Tang.

"And if I may end," intoned the dean, "by quoting the Tao at you all. We have been on a path, a way. We have not, perhaps reached any single, identifiable end but that does not matter. What matters is striving towards ends, what matters is having shared the journey together."

There was loud, rapturous applause, the applause of relief rather than pleasure. Anthony Bridges, singled out by the dean for his special part in the success of the proceedings, was beaming benignly in all directions. His shirt was soaking wet with sweat and his large, spotted handkerchief dangled damply at his side. But his expression was radiant.

Polly who had been mentioned, *en passant*, among the helpful was more than relieved that the conference was over. He never found himself at ease among academic colleagues, wherever they came from. He did not enjoy the kind of limelight that Anthony Bridges soaked up. Crossing the crowded hall where the last farewells were taking place, he wanted nothing more than to slip off to the Gloucester Hotel for a quiet beer.

"Keep up the quest," boomed Professor Korma as Polly passed him, "the quest is all."

Polly nodded a farewell and waved in the direction of the others, making a dash for the gates where the bus was just about to leave. How odd of the dean to refer to Taoism, he thought, comfortably ensconced at the front of the bus. Was he being serious or was he just being ironic? Hardly likely, Meissen was not a man given to light touches or any kind of subtlety—Fiona may have been up to that—he must simply have thought it appropriate to evoke an Oriental spirit at the end of a Western seminar on a sub-tropical island in the South China Sea.

Sitting in the bus, Polly reflected on how Anthony Bridges' suave, soothing condescension had prevented a furious outburst between Professor Korma and Miriam Allsorts. She had launched, with particular malice, into a bitter attack on Korma's pet theories about Coleridge. Anthony Bridges, pontifically ensconced in the chair, clipped her excesses with an amusing, donnish wit that made it impossible for her to protest, or for Korma to butt in without seeming highly ungracious.

This kind of aggressive Western behaviour made Polly admire the *apparent* detachment of the Chinese. Apparent because, as Clarence and Laura insisted, the Chinese were not reticent when they wanted to make a point. Nor did they hesitate to discuss intimacies, sometimes with total strangers. You could be told every detail of a family's illness by someone you had never met before when travelling. The more gruesome, the better.

"But are you supposed to be affected by their revelations?" Polly asked.

"That's just the point," said Clarence, "you may be told all the grisly details, but no one expects you to be particularly upset by them. No one expects you to become involved."

# Chapter 15

A quarter of an hour later, Polly was comfortably installed in his favourite corner of the bar at the Gloucester Hotel. With its rattan chairs and large palm plants, the bar had a cool, old-fashioned feel to it, a quiet retreat away from the maddening noise of Central. It was mid-afternoon; the foreign correspondents who usually provided most of the custom had gone back to their typewriters. A pink-faced, colonial official was sitting in one corner reading an old copy of *The Times;* two Eurasian ladies, in pretty summer dresses, were enjoying colourful cocktails, topped with miniature, brightly coloured paper umbrellas, at their table near the window. To his great relief, there was no one whom Polly knew in the spacious, hotel lounge. He had had enough of having to make polite conversation over the past few days at the seminar.

As Polly sat sipping his beer, enjoying his solitariness, the revolving doors at the entrance swung round and a slim, elegant Chinese lady with long, black hair, dressed in what looked like shiny leather, strode in and marched up confidently to the bar. The colonial official, preening up, rustled his copy of *The Times* slightly.

"Martini, straight up," she said to the barman who in a thrice had thrown the ingredients into a mixer which he proceeded to shake ostentatiously over his shoulder. The Chinese lady sat at the bar where she could see Polly in the mirror. Reaching for her tall triangle-shaped chilled glass; she raised it to his reflection in the gesture of a toast. Polly lifted his own glass in return and smiled. He was amazed at his own audacity with Oriental women. Getting up from his seat, he made his way to the bar, empty glass in hand.

"Fun to see these cocktails mixed," he heard himself saying to the stranger wondering whether she would answer him.

"Great fun," she replied, "why don't you join me? They do an excellent double here."

She muttered something in Cantonese to the barman who deftly produced another glass, matching the first. He placed it on the counter. Stooping down, he poured from his cocktail shaker, just to the right level, then topped off the drink with a stuffed green olive.

"How kind," said Polly hoping that he didn't sound too staid. "Here's to the Gloucester's cocktails."

"To Jimmy's cocktails," she replied as the barman, who had remained quite inscrutable up to that point, nodded the acknowledgement with a grin.

Now that he was up close, Polly could see that the Chinese lady was heavily made-up and might not be as young as her style of fashionable dress had at first suggested. Even so, he admired the smooth, silky texture of her skin, the dark vibrancy of her eyes and her perfect bone structure.

"I'm Cynthia Lee," she said, extending her hand, "you are?"

"I'm John," said Polly.

"Augustus John?" She smiled.

Polly sighed. Was anything in Hong Kong ever spontaneous? Was every encounter always planned? Did anything ever happen by chance?

"So, you know who I am. Perhaps you know me even better than I do myself."

"Only be worried, Mr Polly, if you do not understand others."

"Confucius."

"Yes, Confucius—so beloved to you English, I've never quite understood why."

"Oh, because he is so sensible, so pragmatic," said Polly who, sitting near Cynthia, near enough to catch her scent and imagine her body under the tight blackness that enveloped her, began to feel a flush of excitement coming over him. She made no move as he inched closer to her.

"Plain and sensible, full of common sense, lacking that spirit of mystery that, on the whole, the British don't feel comfortable with," he said with a chuckle.

"Except in detective novels," said Cynthia with a controlled smile on her lips. "But those are very puritanical virtues aren't they—plainness and common sense? Do you think they are enough to get you through the Chinese labyrinth?"

"Good heavens, I don't know about that," said Polly, "much too complicated. Confucius gives Westerners a chance to look at China in a way that they can comprehend."

"As you say, Mr Polly. In a way that they can comprehend."

119

"Call me John," said Polly. "Let's have another drink," he said, beckoning to the barman who was stooped over at the other end of the bar washing glasses. He called out chirpily:

"Two more, Jimmy, on my chit and bring them over to the corner."

Without saying a word, Cynthia got up and walked in front of Polly. Her scent, which he could not quite make out—something pungent but not overpowering—seemed already familiar to him. Who else had used it? He could not remember. Then he noticed her tight, sexy figure, the firm, small breasts, and slim waist that would do credit to a teenage boy, were beginning to grip him as well. She swayed left and right as they crossed the room. They reached the corner and sank into the deep, comfortable chairs, not without glances from the Eurasian ladies. Their cocktails appeared as if by magic.

"Happy days!" said Polly, raising his glass.

"Here's to success," said Cynthia. "Here's to the historical cause."

"Simon Wing has sent you, hasn't he?" Polly said abruptly.

"B4 told me," said Cynthia quietly, "that you are willing to help us. You understand what it is that we want you to do. Your little area of expertise, Mr Polly."

"John, please. Yes, I know what is expected of me. But if capitalism is in its death throes, what's the hurry?"

"We are at a turning point, Mr Polly. Everything is in our favour. We must act now and not at some other time when we may not be so well prepared."

"And the deaths of thousands of innocent bystanders?"

"No commander should fear a reputation for cruelty," said Cynthia coolly. "You must know that as a historian, observing the march of history."

"As a historian, I have knowledge of much suffering," said Polly.

"And do you think about suffering when you get up to your tricks?" She said with a sudden pointedness.

Polly winced. It was almost as if he had been physically struck. He felt humiliated.

"When is it to be?" he said in a dry, impersonal tone.

"Next month," she said without a moment's hesitation. "That will coincide with the Autumn Moon Festival. It will also be about the time of our usual monthly troop manoeuvres. The government here will not expect it. They will think we are posturing as we have always done. But this time it will be for real. While you are doing your bit, which we believe to be highly symbolic, something the ordinary Hong Kong people will understand: our troops will cross the border."

"And how long will it all take?"

"Depends on the resistance. But we think we will take the New Territories and Kowloon in a few days. We have vast numbers, Mr Polly, and they are eager for action."

Polly drained the rest of his cocktail in one gulp. Suddenly he started to feel cold. He was developing the shivers. Had the air-conditioning been turned up? What was the sharp pain he felt in the pit of his stomach?

Cynthia Lee had finished her drink. Polly could not help noticing her hands as she lowered her glass to the table. He had the urge to stuff her fingers in his mouth and lick them, one at a time. Instead, he leaned forward and covered her hand with his larger one, looking into her dark, expressionless eyes. She let her hand rest in his, then after a few moments, withdrew it.

"If everything goes well and you are successful, the rewards will be great, Mr Polly. We do not forget those who have helped us. You will be honoured; you will be taken under the jurisdiction of the Committee Supervising Distinguished Foreigners."

"Foreigners, not devils?" Polly said.

"Those who have helped the cause gain honorary status, Mr Polly. They are becoming honorary Chinese."

Polly remained silent. He found Cynthia's last comment unconvincing, even absurd. Foreigners becoming Chinese, that was a likely tale! When had the Chinese ever admitted equality with foreigners, even helpful ones? They were the supreme racists, every bit as xenophobic as the colonists like Alistair Crowley who governed the 'fragrant harbour' with such casual arrogance.

Polly looked at Cynthia Lee again. He tried hard to read her thoughts. But there wasn't the slightest hint of what she might be thinking in her placid, cool expression. It was impossible to penetrate those layers of Chinese-ness.

"I must be going now, Mr Polly," she said suddenly, interrupting his thoughts. "From now on, you will be dealing with me. I'll be in touch at the beginning of the week. Let me know if there is anything you need when I call you."

"That will be a pleasure," said Polly with barely concealed salaciousness.

Cynthia had got up, picked up her shiny leather handbag with its long strap, flung it over her shoulder, and without another word, disappeared out of the room. Downing the last of his drink, Polly stood, nodded at the barman who was mixing another cocktail in his showman-like way and left the bar. When he was outside the front door of the Gloucester Hotel, he saw that night was rapidly falling and there was the faintest suggestion of coolness. Polly decided to walk home, an eccentric thing for a European to do in Hong Kong where no one walked—except on a golf course—even though the streets were safe thanks to a constant police presence.

The sky was a brilliant pink that night, still streaked with some blue and spangled with stars like confetti at a wedding. Polly stopped to gaze down at the harbour, magnificent with its thousands of coloured lights. Ships, ferries and junks were bouncing slightly on the waves. The air was warm, filled with the lush, intoxicating smell of jasmine; from the green slopes of the Peak, the cicadas croaked, and insects buzzed past in the dark. How could it be that all this was transient, that at any moment it might all be swept away?

Polly turned away from the blazing scene in front of him and continued his walk, now just passing Ah Chueng's. In the deep recesses of the shop, a light was flickering, and Polly could hear the thin, hermaphroditic wail of the Chinese male opera singer on a wireless, a tuneless whine to his English ears. Fiona Meissen had been right when she said in the garden that there was no harmony in their music.

And thinking of Fiona Meissen reminded Polly of Cynthia Lee. God! Was she a mirage too, without firm breasts to fondle or silky slender, buttocks to glide over with gentle hands? How maddening it was to think of these women. How contradictory everything was, how upside down. Hadn't the poet said, *The East has all the time, the West has none*? But it was Cynthia who acted as if there was no time left while Fiona, calm and composed, appeared to have all the time in the world.

Polly reached the door of No.3. He had crossed the campus without seeing anyone. He stepped into the dark hall, not putting on the light in case anyone was watching the house and could see him entering. In the pitch black, he walked up the stairs. Entering his study, he switched on a dim nightlight and sat down.

It was warm in the room as the blinds had been closed. Polly could feel himself sweating. He slithered down into the depth of a low rattan chair, flicking off his cuff links which crashed noisily onto the bare, parquet floor. In a few minutes, he was groaning with pleasure as he worked vigorously on himself, an image of Cynthia Lee, naked but for a thin gauze veil drawn tightly over her breasts, burning in his mind. The whirring of the ceiling fan was all that could be heard above his panting.

# Chapter 16

When Polly woke up, it was to the insistent pealing of the telephone. Momentarily, he did not know where he was. His head felt heavy, his limbs were sore. It was with difficulty that he found the receiver.

"So, Polly you *are* there," cooed the sumptuous voice of Anthony Bridges. "You haven't forgotten that the Pryce-Joneses are giving a party for university staff involved in the seminar, have you?"

Polly had not forgotten but he had tried hard to put the event out of his mind. However, he knew that he wouldn't get away with it. In Hong Kong, it was impossible to escape social obligations. Sir Edwin Pyrce-Jones, a taipan who worked for the illustrious firm of Jardine Matheson, was one of the few businessmen who supported the university—the dean had played the old college card hard in his case—so an invitation to cocktails at his Peak mansion was a three-line whip occasion.

"No, I haven't forgotten," said Polly truthfully, his mouth dry and throat sore as if the three or four afternoon cocktails with Cynthia Lee had been a bottle.

"What time do we have to leave?"

"In about half-an-hour. I say, you sound a bit odd, Polly, are you alright?"

"Yes, I'm fine," said Polly, this time untruthfully. "How are we going to get there?"

"Oh, let's take a taxi," said Anthony Bridges expansively. "I don't want to drive over the cliffs on the way back. Or shall we scrounge a lift with the Meissens?"

"No, let's go by taxi," said Polly at once.

The last thing he felt like was a lecture from the dean on the way up the peak. The party was going to be a trying affair without that prelude.

"I'll be with you in twenty minutes, let me jump into the shower."

He hung up abruptly.

Forty minutes later, Anthony Bridges and Polly were wending along the snake-like road up to the Peak. There was a strong scent of oleander in the air; the stars covered the sky in a twinkling carpet. It was a dazzling, tropical night.

"Tell me, Anthony," said Polly, desperate to take his mind off Cynthia Lee "what do you make, as a philosopher of course, of the connection between an intellectual theory such as Marxism and actual revolutionary events, like Mao and the Red Army and all that?"

"God, what a question to ask, Polly, as we make our way to the Pryce-Joneses. Still," he smirked, "better now than at the residence where her ladyship has arranged all the books according to size rather than content!"

Both dons grinned in the back seat of the taxi. At the last gathering, Sir Edwin had taken the group into the library, a room with a magnificent round alcove sweeping majestically out of the side of the house, giving a dramatic view of the harbour. The shelves that ran from floor to ceiling were lined with books. Polly looked closely at them and was puzzled to find an odd mix of subjects. Old company ledgers, bound in fine leather, were thrown next to books about exotic birds and wildlife and higgledy-piggledy among them were novels of the moment. Serious history seemed to be absent altogether. When Mr Polly asked about the arrangement of the books on the shelves, Anthea Pryce-Jones had replied airily, "Oh, according to size, Polly. I'm surprised you, of all people, should ask about arranging books."

Polly glanced at Anthony Bridges, but he had turned away to avoid his gaze.

Instead, with consummate bad faith, Anthony Bridges said breezily.

"And easier for the servants to dust."

"Quite," said Anthea Pryce-Jones sweeping out of the room to greet newly arrived guests.

"Well, Anthony?" Polly said, still waiting for the philosopher's reply to his question about theory and reality.

"It's a difficult question to answer," said Anthony. "It's not only a matter of measuring to see what degree of approximation the activities of the Communists have had to any recognisable Marxist-Leninist theory—that's something that I would rather leave to you historians. No, it raises the matter of the relationship between ideas and action, cognitive processes in the human brain and the jumble of events that your lot favour with the name 'history'."

"That's the part I'm asking about," said Polly.

"Well, Polly, you know the school of philosophy to which I belong. What I am saying is that the sentence 'Ideas are linked to action' is a synthetic statement, something that needs to be measured by empirical means in the way that you do as a historian. But if you are asking whether I see an intrinsic logical connection between the ideas and action, something that might be of an analytic nature, then the answer is no. I see no logical connection."

"Does that mean that anyone acting as a revolutionary has no guide, no certainty about the validity of his motives?"

"Motives! Good God, Polly! I am talking about the quality of statements and the way we can test their meaning. That has nothing to do with human motivation, a subject I would embark upon with trepidation."

"That's the trouble with contemporary philosophy," sighed Polly. "It doesn't get you anywhere near answering the really important questions of history, the whys."

"But it keeps you away from nonsense," said Anthony Bridges. Then as an afterthought, he added smugly "Or rather it makes you recognise nonsense for what it is—an expression of emotion, therefore of no logical interest."

Polly did not reply. As the taxi continued taking the hazardous bends of the hill, he lapsed into his own thoughts. Where does that lead one in reaching 'ultimate history?' What did it say about the activities of Simon Wing and Cynthia Lee in which he now conspired? They would, of course, simply sneer at such intellectual dithering. For them, the important thing was to challenge the status quo.

Suddenly there was a grating noise as the taxi swung off the road onto the long gravel drive that led up to the Pryce-Jones's, an entrance that might have been in the hidden depths of the Wiltshire countryside, rather than in crowded Hong Kong. Trees lined the route to give as much shade as possible; pretty, luscious tropical flowers were planted at intervals in large, Chinese garden pots. Tennis courts and a swimming pool lay discreetly hidden to the side. Manicured green lawns completed the picture of an ideally laid-out space.

Out of the car window, Polly stared at the Pryce-Jones's estate in wonder. What must it be like to live in this manner on a daily basis? He mused to himself. Limousines arrived with important guests to daily cocktail parties, social events arranged around the tennis courts, the swimming pool, and a marquee that was put up and taken down at the slightest whim of Lady Pryce-Jones. Servants of every grade and type from the number one cook, with all his status and importance to the humblest boy who picked up the tennis balls, scattered insouciantly by guests into the bushes. And there in the middle of it all, sailed Anthea Pryce-Jones, always impeccably coiffured, tastefully rather than lavishly dressed, irrepressibly bubbling, a certain condescension always at hand to deal with guests not quite from the right drawer, or with the Chinese, however grand, to remind them of their place in the Crown colony. Anthea in her chiffon dress, her left shoulder draped with a long scarf in the Roman style, ready by mid-morning to do battle with the world. What a formidable, tireless, relentless, capable *grande dame*!

"Come in, gentlemen, come in," she commanded as they stepped out of their taxi, "before you get hot. It's a terribly muggy evening, come in, it's deliciously cool inside."

Polly and Anthony Bridges were led into the house by number one (of twelve) imposing house-boys who, like the rest, were dressed in a starched white jacket with gleaming brass buttons. They strode down the long hall, with its great display of Japanese Imari and old Chinese lacquer, into the vast, oval ballroom where upward of a hundred guests were already downing champagne and snatching up canapés under the radiant constellation of enormous, Venetian candelabra. In the far corner of the room, on an elevated parquet platform, a string quartet was smoothly playing Mantovani numbers.

Members of the Pryce-Jones's staff stood at intervals, like sentinels, carrying large silver platters. Polly had never seen silver of this size before he came to Hong Kong but then, as Laura Li tartly observed, there was no shortage of hands to clean and polish it. Mounds of thinly cut sandwiches, the edges taken off; vast Pacific prawns pierced with Jardine Matheson daggers, canapés of the most exotic types, weighed down the huge platters.

Polly and Anthony Bridges skirted past the circle surrounding Sir Reginald, the governor, in his evening whites, closely chaperoned by Alistair Crowley, spruced and brushed to the nines. In another group was the governor's wife, Lady Fogerty in a satin dress with patterned camellia flowers, the colonial secretary, a dour-looking man with thin lips, and the company chairman's glamorous French wife who had caused a great stir by arriving in a *chueng sam*, tightly fitted to her very slim figure. Here and there was a Chinese face. They were probably all members of the Lam tribe, Polly thought.

Anthony Bridges, struggling with several sandwiches and a tall glass of champagne, still managed to talk without pause.

"Look at that little group over there," he said in a tone discreet by his standards, "what must their combined wealth amount to?"

"I can't imagine," said Polly, gulping down his drink. "But the Fogertys aren't wealthy, just grand, aren't they?"

"Good heavens, Polly, don't you know anything? Lady Fogerty is a cousin of the Andropolos, the great ship-owners, among the richest people in the world."

Polly blinked. He was dazzled by the flash of a silver tureen that was wheeled past them. He thought of the old, wizened lady who always hung about outside the university gates with her begging bowl, he thought of the emaciated messenger at Ah Chueng's, the hollow-cheeked rickshaw coolies at the Star Ferry, the ragged children screaming in the nearby tenement in Wanchai when he had visited the printer's shop in preparation for the seminar. Simon Wing and Cynthia Lee were right—there had to be radical change, there had to be.

"It must all go," he said aloud.

"But not all at once," said Anthony Bridges, thinking that Polly was referring to the vessels of champagne, the tables groaning with food. Helping himself to another large glass, he disappeared into the crowd, determined to pin down Alistair Crowley to hear the latest political gossip. Polly looked around at the throngs of guests, all apparently effortlessly engaged in social banter. To his delight, he spotted the elegant figure of Fiona Meissen apparently on her own. Just as he looked at her, she caught sight of him and smiling broadly, came across to talk.

"Mr Polly," she said in a mock-ceremonious manner, "what a pleasure to see you."

As she came nearer, her ever-fragrant presence registered in his nose.

"Fiona how nice to see someone I know," said Polly narrowly avoiding a plump, be-sashed lady whose plate of piled-high *hors d'oeuvres* almost flew into the air.

"How did the seminar go?"

"Oh, very well, Fiona. Nothing untoward happened. No incidents."

"What a pity," said Fiona and looking straight at each other, they both burst into laughter.

"That fellow Korma," said Fiona. "I simply can't stand him. One of George's Oxford friends—an insufferable bore as far as I am concerned."

"Well, he's certainly not the easiest man to understand," volunteered Polly, "an idealist view of life."

"Idealist," spluttered Fiona, choking for a moment over the paprika that had been dusted on her cucumber sandwich.

"I've heard that he goes about from one conference to another and virtually lives on the allowances he gets for attending them."

"Oh, I meant in a philosophical sense," said Polly, "idealist as opposed to empiricist."

"Stuff and nonsense, Polly. He's a crook. You can see it in his eyes, my dear."

She turned to face Polly squarely—how pretty her deep blue eyes were.

"He never does that, never looks at you properly. Always a bad sign. Quite untrustworthy, I tell you."

Polly said nothing. Instead, he beckoned to a waiter to bring them another cocktail each. When the fine, crystal glasses, miraculously chilled, were in their hands, he spoke again.

"Fiona, do you think that one can act honestly for the public good?"

"The public good?" Fiona said quizzically. "You mean in politics?"

Polly nodded.

"Oh, of course, one can," she said confidently, "but the difficulty is that you never really know what will come of it."

"You mean the effect of your action?"

It was Fiona's turn to nod.

"Yes, take the example of the Communists. I'm sure they started with the best of intentions. But now…"

Intentions again thought Polly to himself, but this time, just taken for granted, not brooded over or analysed in an academic way.

"And now?"

"Well, I don't think anyone believes all that idealistic claptrap any longer. They might have believed it once. But now it's become a power game. Things have simply changed."

"Or not so simply," said Polly.

Fiona smiled at his cleverness, but her thoughts had moved on.

"Funny, Polly, here we are talking about change again. Remember at Ah Chueng's, when I asked you about infidelity?"

Polly reddened. The plump lady with the brightly coloured sash cocked her ear slightly on hearing the word infidelity. The Pryce-Jones's cocktail parties were rich pastures for gossip gatherers and rumour mongers.

"Yes, I do," he said. "I suppose it's a paradox of my profession—concerned with the past, but not as a dead thing, but as something that changes even as we look at it."

"I think you're very sweet, Polly," said Fiona, and before he could stutter in response, she had leaned over, giving him a gentle, sisterly peck on the cheek. Then she moved off abruptly into the swirl of the other guests. She too had a duty to circulate and to speak up for the university.

Polly stood still, glass in hand and closed his eyes. He imagined that he could still feel Fiona Meissen's lips on his cheek, could still sense the thickening perfume of the air as she came nearer, hear the crinkle of her dress as she moved towards him for that one, swift, moment of contact, so light, so airy that it was possible that it had not happened at all. But Polly knew that it had happened, as surely as Caesar had invaded Britain, as surely as a thousand species of tulip had been cultivated for the Ottoman sultans at the Sublime Porte, as surely as the Chinese calligraphers had practised their arts over all those centuries. However much, or little was the significance of Fiona Meissen's peck, it had happened and now, Polly, as a historian had decided to select it as an important fact in the true history of Mr Polly. He closed his eyes and saw a scene in Wanchai.

Simon Wing and Cynthia Lee sat near the door to avoid the smoky interior of a dingy Wanchai restaurant. They were soon joined by Laura Li and Clarence Lam who ordered tea and then waited in silence. After a few minutes, Laura began speaking in fluent Mandarin.

"You three may be convinced," she said, "but I am not. Can we take the risk of leaving such an important part of the mission to a half-witted academic?"

Clarence intervened at once.

"Please, Laura, Mr Polly may be eccentric, but he is not half-witted."

"Leaving that aside," said Simon Wing, "and I must say I did not get the idea that he was a fool at all, Laura has a point. The whole mission could be aborted if that part of it goes wrong. What do you think, Cynthia?"

Cynthia did not answer at once. Instead, she spread out her fingers, in a fan-like movement, on the table.

"He will be alright," she said, stroking her own arm, "once he has tasted our special, Chinese offerings…"

Polly opened his eyes again to see Anthony Bridges standing in front of him.

"Polly, are you alright? You looked a bit odd. The dean noticed and asked me to come over and check. We wouldn't want a repeat of the launch picnic episode here!"

"No, I am fine," said Polly, "there's no buzz in my head, just a whiff of Wanchai in the air."

Anthony Bridges nodded as if he understood. In fact, he hadn't any idea what Polly was talking about. But his colleague's looks reassured him.

"We need to circulate. Come on, Polly; let's frighten those Greeks over there with a few words in their ancient tongue."

Polly followed Anthony Bridges across the room. The Greek ship-owners stood in a semi-circle. Polly tried to read what was on their minds from their expressions, but it was not easy. He noticed a thick-set young man who looked dour until a smile suddenly lit up his whole face. Anthony Bridges was regaling them in Greek; they clearly had difficulty understanding though they nodded appreciatively. Polly was not listening to the conversation; he would have been hard-pressed even to say which language was being spoken. Instead, he watched everything through gestures, tones of voice and body movements.

And in his mind's eye, he could not escape the image of Cynthia Lee with her triangular, pale face, her skin that had the pallor of white flowers, her slim waist and slender hips, the firm round bosoms that he wanted to bite. And throughout the rest of that evening and into the next morning when the string quartet was replaced by a dance band and couples glided around the enormous oval room with its tall veranda doors flung open to the starry night, Polly could think of nothing else except the curved lines of Cynthia, her sensuous, small mouth, the hidden treasures of her body…

# Chapter 17

By the time Polly and Anthony Bridges left the Pryce-Jones party, it was three in the morning. Most of the other guests had left except for a hard core of drinkers, members of the racing set. They had retreated to a huddle on the veranda where the last waiter continued to serve them. The Pryce-Joneses had retired, bidding their guests farewell and indicating that they could stay so long as the drink lasted.

Anthony Bridges was the worst for wear, but Polly was quite sober. He and Fiona Meissen had been most modest in drinking. It seemed that once he had the strong vision of Cynthia Lee, his need for drink had diminished. His head was so clear that it felt as if he had taken aspirin.

As the two men waited for their taxi at the grand entrance, the warm air enveloped them. The only sounds to be heard were the wings of bats circling above them and the high-pitched buzzing of the cicadas. A light mist hung over the manicured lawn.

Soon they were in a taxi screeching down the sweeping driveway that led up to the mansion. As their taxi rounded a bend to descend into the lower levels, Polly asked the young driver to stop so suddenly that the wheels of the car skidded onto the wide, cobbled nullah that ran on the side of the tarmac. Anthony Bridges started up from his slumped position on the back seat.

"Polly, Polly, what…"

"Anthony, the driver will take you home. I'm getting out here. I desperately need some fresh air and I'll walk home."

"Very well, old boy," said Anthony Bridges in a sing-song voice, "seez you latcher," and in a thrice, he had fallen back to sleep.

Polly took out his wallet and handed the taxi driver a ten-dollar bill, told him Anthony Bridges' address and gave him the front door key.

"Go to Number 7, University Drive," he said to the man who nodded. "Make sure he gets into the house."

The man nodded again showing no surprise as if this was the way that all *gweilos*—foreign devils—behaved. How many times had he had to deal with foreigners who could hardly get out of the taxi due to excess alcohol? He looked in the mirror to check that Anthony Bridges was asleep.

How fortunate to be in Hong Kong, thought Polly. Probably the only city in the world where such a thing could be done safely. And all because of the immense power of figures like Chief Inspector Chan. The security of the police state.

Polly got out of the taxi and stood motionless for a few minutes, inhaling the intoxicating air, scented with frangipani. He decided on a long, slow walk. As he strolled off, there was a light breeze, the stars still shone in their place and the only sound to be heard was the distant barking of a dog. Taking a path that led over the hills, he began his descent to the small bay, nestling in the moonlight below. The mist of the Peak had vanished. Polly was bathed in the profuse, white beams of the moon. His heart was beating with excitement. He could hear the chugging of a boat's engine, either fishermen returning with a catch or smugglers from Macao.

From the roadside, Polly scrambled over some rocks, careful not to slip. Once he had reached the beach, with its welcoming warm sand, he pulled off his black tie with a quick tug. Then he took off his shoes and socks, shirt and trousers and threw them in a heap. Finally, Polly pulled off his underpants—a snazzy silk pair that he had found in the Lane Crawford sale. He stood naked, gazing out at the bay. Everything was quiet; the boat had disappeared around the rocks at the edge of the bay. It was a scene of utter tranquillity.

Polly ran towards the sea and plunged in. He felt the delicious, warm water break over his back as he swam a steady breaststroke further and further out. Lying on his back and floating in the water, Polly squirted a fountain of water into the air. What a joy to swim in the tropics: the warmth of the water, the sweet scent of the darkness and no one around to disturb the peace. Floating gently for a few minutes, Polly let himself roll over and then glided slowly towards the raft, dark and bobbing gently in the current. He hauled himself onto the swaying planks and sat, facing the shore, with his feet in the water.

Sitting in the moonlight, calm Polly began to think of all that had happened to him since he left his dreary life in London for the glitz of Hong Kong. Not that he was entirely at home in colonial life. It seemed somehow too privileged. On the other hand, it was easy to slip into a routine where there was nothing to irritate him except Ah Hing's tea. Wonderful, respectful students—with the exception of Laura Li—excursions for dim sum, smart hotel bars, launch picnics to the unspoilt islands around. And now it was all under threat. Chief Inspector Chan was on to him. A slip and it would all be over. Alistair Crowley would be triumphant.

Perched on the raft, Polly looked towards the beach, but could not see well as the reflected rays of the moon shone on him. Was that a figure near his bundle of clothes? He tried to strain his eyes to see better, but the moon slipped in behind a cloud. Could it be a woman's figure, a slim Oriental one, or perhaps it was a boy? He could not see properly. Standing up quickly, Polly dived off the raft and swam forward in a rapid crawl, getting near the beach in a few minutes. As he waded ashore in the shallow water, some seaweed, slimy and smelly, clung to his foot. Looking towards the spot where he had left his clothes, he could see behind the clump they formed, some tall canes of bamboo swaying in the light breeze. Nobody was to be seen.

# Chapter 18

By morning, Polly had forgotten all about the Pryce-Jones' party. Suddenly, he was aware of a new sensation within himself. He noticed that his buzzing headaches, those bouts of vertiginous and painful attacks that he had been subject to, and which occurred at the most awkward moments, had entirely disappeared. Polly did not feel calm, in fact, quite the reverse, the decisions and episodes of the last weeks had left him in a state of excited expectancy, an uncertainty about the future which although unsettling, at the same time added a new sense of zest and vibrancy to his life.

Flashes from the past continued to unsettle him. The figure of Chief Inspector Chan, always set in that scene in his office, at the desk, questioning Polly so suavely but with an undertone of menace, would not go away. Past and present mingled and meshed together in his mind. He felt as if his whole life was suddenly being relived at one moment, at a moment when all the differing accounts of his behaviour would have to be settled.

Polly's sense of excitement, at the idea that the future was going to be dramatic, was accompanied by a steady confidence that amounted to a kind of fatalism. He went about his daily tasks as if nothing had happened, but within himself, he knew that, at any moment, at the lifting of the morning mist from the peak, his life could be irrevocably changed. That feeling gave him a sense of buoyant expectancy, of subdued excitement, but momentarily there was a flicker of regret, a feeling that it was better to lurk in the mists of the present, to stumble along half-seeing, than to endure the stark, cold light of the heroic.

Was he really made for such a role? Polly knew that meeting Cynthia Lee had stimulated his newly-found *élan*. He understood the dangers of committing himself to something that was a mere sexual infatuation, an entirely transient experience. From the beginning of their affair, he had noticed something detached about Cynthia's manner. Even at the moment of greatest passion, when their bodies were violently entwined in heated love-making, he sensed that she only pretended to lose control, that underneath everything, a strong, stern will dominated her every physical response. Yet search though he might through the magazines of his soul, he could not find the equivalent of the sensations that he was experiencing; he could not match their colour or their vividness. Polly knew that there was no future in their relationship, but its presence, forceful, energising, even painful, filled his entire being. A fleeting infatuation had turned into obsession.

Maud Manderley Simpson! Suddenly the clear image of Maud came into Polly's mind, clearer than it had been for a long time. What had he ever seen in her? Mousy-haired and plain, never smart or even near smartness. Maud so dowdy, so middle-aged in her youth, had nevertheless been kind to him. Or had she just been drawn to his vulnerability, moved by a desire to sort out his absent-minded, seedy bachelor existence?

Polly remembered those solitary, grey days. There was a bleak poetry about them that matched the cold, harsh stone of the Senate House. There in the musty library corridors, he shuffled through life, nothing exciting or glamorous ever touched him. His daily routine was the same. It began with a brisk morning run from Canterbury Gardens along to Judd Street, then a sharp right past the camera shop that seemed permanently closed and, in a great curving arc, back to Russell Square. In summer he varied the pattern somewhat and gave up the run, instead tumbling down the slippery, tiled stairs to the Union pool, through the turnstile that made one feel like an animal being counted entering a pen. Only when he slipped into the deliciously cool, chlorine-misted water did he gain a sense of liberation and experience a feeling of freedom that he imagined was like gliding through ether.

And then there were the visits to Maud. Her thick-set glasses always hid any expression in her eyes, the deathly pallor of her skin. Nothing to catch the eye, nothing to indicate anything human until she smiled, and a warm glowing smile that revealed quite unexpected and immaculate teeth. How the smile transformed the face, how the years rolled off her, how much Polly wanted to rest his head on her bosom and allow her to stroke his hair. What Polly did not understand— and how could he, a man whose only companions were silent books?—was the insufficiency of Maud's warmth, however devouring its quality was. Maud's instinct was a relentless, automatic feature of her character, there to be turned up and down like a gas fire, it was not love, it was not even affection. It was pure desire.

And then the marriage, married life. Dreariness itself even in recollection. A poetic grey exchanged for a suburban grey—the small house at the end of the tube line; Polly setting out for the library with his packed sandwiches, always the same, never varied, returning at night to the garishly bright electric fire logs, as artificial as the feeling between husband and wife. Maud out in the afternoon, working in the local council, penny-pinched, tatty, a half-etched life. Days off from work were even more dreadful because they were thrown together with nothing to say, unable to decide what to do with their leisure which everyone else glowed about and said was so precious.

It lasted six months. It should have lasted less. One windy March day, Polly came home in the afternoon, feeling cowardly, barely able to carry out his plan. Packing a few things, he left a note on the kitchen table in the place where they always left notes.

*Dear Maud,*

*I don't think this will come as a surprise. I think it's better if we spend a bit of time apart. I have collected some things and I will arrange for someone to come to get the rest over the weekend. Everything will be paid, as usual, through the bank so you don't need to worry about all that. I'm awfully sorry, darling.*

He hesitated over the word 'darling' but then thought that it didn't really matter. He could afford to be intimate as he planned not to see her again. At the bottom of the note, he quickly scribbled his name which, for an inexplicable reason he had written in neat, printed capitals. Clutching his leather bag, he rushed out of the house towards the tube. So simple it seemed to step out of life.

And now he was at the other end of the world, involved with another woman who could hardly be more different from Maud. Cynthia with her self-confidence, her chic and her glamorous job as a newspaper correspondent; the model of the determined career woman.

A pattern had soon developed in their affair. Each week they would meet either in the bar of the Gloucester Hotel, because Cynthia worked just nearby, or in the upstairs tea room of Lane Crawford, with its subdued lights and air-conditioned modernity.

"Always open, always visible," said Cynthia, "don't you know, Polly, that the best place to have a secret conversation is in the middle of a cocktail party?"

After their drink, they would take a taxi to Macdonnell Road where Cynthia lived in a spacious flat, tastefully decorated with Blackwood furniture and sumptuous, Peking carpets. There they had more drinks on the oval balcony, looking down to the magnificent harbour. Soon Cynthia would lead Polly indoors and slipping out of her *chueng sam*, pull him onto the rich, yellow, satin cushions of a great opium bed which stood ornamentally at one end of the room. There on the old wooden boards that would have housed a smoker and his pipes, Polly lost himself in Cynthia, inhaling over and again her fragrance of caraway and plunging ever more deeply into the world of bright stars and meteors that he saw when his eyes were firmly closed.

The weeks slipped by deliciously, but too quickly for Polly. One day, after a session on the opium bed Cynthia looked more pensive than usual. Her hair fell in long strands over her shoulders.

"What's the matter?" Polly asked though he already knew what the answer would be.

"It's getting near the time, Polly," said Cynthia in a dry, low voice.

"How long?" He said, dreading to hear the reply.

"In ten days', time," she answered, "to coincide with the Moon Festival."

Polly started. A mere ten days. He had been putting all thoughts of what was to happen out of his mind. He hardly dared to go to the Hong Kong & Shanghai Bank any longer to deposit or withdraw sums, always modest, from his account. On the last occasion he had entered the vast bronze doors, passed the great stone lions and walked across the marble expanses of the interior with its elegant art deco frieze high up around the wall, he had felt distinctly nervous. It was as if, at any moment, one of the smart security guards, in their special uniform, would come over and ask him to step into the manager's office for a 'chat'. In fact, it was an English voice that made him jump—Alistair Crowley, slipping out of the Securities Section with a self-satisfied smirk on his face, spotted him and called out his name.

"Sorry to startle you, old boy. You looked as if you were coming to rob the old HK & S," he said in a mock-jocular tone.

Polly tried to recover his composure.

"Academic pay hasn't yet reduced me to that yet," he said, pleased that he had managed to counter Alistair Crowley's facetiousness. Alistair Crowley smiled in a non-committal way. There was more than a whiff of condescension in his manner which Polly did not like, indeed which he found offensive.

Polly knew only too well what the senior officials at the Colonial Secretariat thought of people like him: dangerous intellectuals, as likely to be on the other side as on the home side, utterly unreliable. Alistair Crowley gave Polly a curt nod and, putting on his Panama hat, strode out of the great doors of the bank.

Polly gazed at Cynthia again as she sat inscrutably on the opium bed.

"What about a few days in Macao?" He said. "It may be our last chance."

"Why not?" Cynthia said. "I could go the day after tomorrow. Do you want me to make bookings?"

Polly nodded. He was always impressed by Cynthia's speed in making up her mind. No doubts, no dilly-dallying, just getting on with it.

# Chapter 19

Two days later, Polly was in another taxi, this time with Cynthia, on the way to the Macao Ferry Pier. The driver, having to swerve violently to miss an old beggar, was swearing volubly in Cantonese which Polly knew was the foulest language in the world when it came to cursing. The beggar jumped onto the pavement and stood, staring at them in silence.

"I suppose these people will be better off when things change?" Polly said pointing at the beggar and wanting to break the awkward silence that had fallen over them.

"They won't be on the streets if that's what you mean," said Cynthia grimly. Then she muttered in Cantonese to the driver who stopped his whining at once.

"Polly, we are almost at the pier. The ferry sails in fifteen minutes, have you got your passport, and the tickets?"

Polly took out a travel folder as the taxi screeched up to the pier entrance.

"What do we do, Cynthia, if we see anyone we know?"

"Behave normally," she said. "Look, my dear, everyone knows we are having an affair. It's done the rounds. The Pryce-Joneses have stopped inviting me to their parties, a sure sign that they know a 'native' woman like me is corrupting an innocent, 'foreign devil' like you. It's just as we planned—perfect cover for collaboration."

Polly did not reply. He felt Cynthia's remarks stabbing deeply in his chest. So, there was nothing more to it than that? An affair, widely broadcast to throw people off the scent that they were really conspirators. Discussing secrets in the middle of cocktail parties. Shocking the Pryce-Joneses deliberately. Everything was part of the plan. Nothing spontaneous or unexpected, nothing romantic about their attachment.

Once through the Immigration Hall, a long dreary shed-like building as unfriendly then in mid-afternoon as it might be at three in the morning, they embarked on the ferry, making their way to the front bar. Cynthia was immaculate in her travelling outfit, no doubt the latest in French or Italian design, thought Polly. She had changed her hairstyle, now sporting a fashionable fringe which gave more prominence to the high cheekbones and jet-black lashes of her eyes. She looked pretty, alert and ready for any adventure. Polly was besotted by her body fragrance, the gestures of her hands, and the intonation of her voice. Knowing that these were elusive, evanescent qualities that could not be captured, or tied down, he wanted them more, and his demand for them became insistent. Cynthia was a mirage as much as a person. But he no longer cared.

For four hours, the ferry slid over the water, green and frothing. In the distance, were the dark shapes of islands, like creatures sleeping on the surface of the water; above the afternoon sky was brilliant and cloudless. The sound of the ferry's engines chugging them along and the lapping of the waves on its sides was reassuring.

Taking their drinks onto the deck, they gazed out at the disappearing horizon. It was a smooth passage, an escape from the mad bustle of the city. Polly was relieved to find that there was no one on board whom they recognised to disturb their peace. Not even a member of the Lam tribe. Before long, from the deck railings, they could see the choppy water turn muddy brown. The outline of the city began to appear. A church perched on one hill; an imposing colonial building on another. And as the boat swung round, the majestic ruins of São Paolo, only the façade still standing, came into view. All that remained of the Jesuit legacy. Polly pointed it out with his right hand while his left arm rested on Cynthia's waist.

On the distant horizon was the darkness of China.

"And will they ever bother with this sleepy little backwater?" Polly said.

Cynthia frowned and withdrew from Polly's grip. He realised that she was annoyed at his loose talk, even there on the deck where they were alone with no one to overhear them or have the faintest idea of what they meant. Polly watched the ferry dock at the Macao Pier, soaked in a hazy afternoon sun. How quiet and peaceful it seemed after Hong Kong. A solitary sailor ready to catch the rope to tie them up, a few coolies on the ground ready to clamber aboard. No crowds, no bustle. Only the faint murmur of a radio playing Chinese opera and the strange, Slavonic-sounding swishes of the Portuguese Immigration officials chatting and smoking on the pier, carried across the water.

A tricycle took them up to their hotel, the rambling old Bela Vista with its fine view over the Praia Grande and the muddy waters of the estuary beyond.

Polly felt at home in the dark, sombre building which had not changed in decades. Led up to the first floor, they passed the great battle scene on the landing where an ethereal King Sebastião of Portugal, already rising in the air, looked down sadly on the dead, the flower of his nobility, strewn on the bloody field below. There was a strange, yellow glow behind the king's head, giving him the luminous quality that the artist had intended. Just next to the painting was the door to their room which was large and cool, with large French windows that led onto a balcony with old Chinese pots in rustic yellow and dragons imposed in deep brown on their rims.

Polly sat on the balcony watching the setting sun. He heard Cynthia dealing with the room boy who had brought their drinks. Then she came out briefly, placing the tray on the table next to him and went back inside. The evening ferry was leaving for Hong Kong, slipping out again into the middle of the bay. The sails of junks could be seen silhouetted against the setting sun. Polly sipped his drink and looked down at the waterfront. He could hear Cynthia moving about the room, preparing herself for the evening.

Polly did not feel at ease. He knew that Cynthia was preoccupied with the future. A froideur had crept into her manner; her easy smile had gone. Polly knew that there had always been some reserve, but it had seemed to disappear as their relationship became more physically serious. Or had he just imagined that it had? Polly tried to recall each of his meetings with Cynthia. There had been so many. Had her manner changed on one particular occasion? He could not recall it. Instead, he could only remember scenes of passionate lovemaking on the opium bed, on the carpeted floor of her flat and even on the cold tiles of the hallway which cooled his back as he lay panting for breath. No one could deny her frenzy in copulation, the deep scratches and bites that she left on him, the screaming that he thought would bring someone to the door. But what of her feelings, had they ever matched the desire?

Polly did not feel that they made good company that evening. A delightful coolness had fallen over Macao as he watched the junks sail gracefully into the bay, taking advantage of a light wind. At dinner, he was taciturn while Cynthia surveyed the courses of Chinese food brought to the round table, with an indifferent stare. The fun had gone out of their liaison; it was now tainted with a feeling of being past its time. Polly sensed that Cynthia recognised this as clearly as he did. But unlike him, she did not care. She had enjoyed the excitement of making love to a 'foreign devil', but she had never been seduced by him. She had certainly never fallen in love.

Cynthia stared at Polly across the dinner table which had now been cleared of all the dishes and wiped clean for tea. Her only thought was whether he would go through with it, whether, in a week's time he would perform a task so vital to the success of the whole operation. She looked at his face, still pale after years in the tropics, the grey-green eyes, intelligent and now filled with an expression—of what? Was it anticipation, was it apprehension? She found it impossible to determine.

She thought about him after they had sex, lying on his back, smoking a cigarette, staring into space. He seemed so weak, so impotent. How easily men could be controlled. Always posturing as the strong ones, apparently brave and forward, in fact cringing in the shadow of a woman—mother, wife, mistress— whose influence came from stronger will-power, an ability to sustain misfortunes, setbacks, even calamities, and rise from them with renewed strength. Cynthia had learnt all these lessons as a girl in Suchow, watching her great-aunt control a household of men, second uncles, third cousins, all jostling for pre-eminence. Great-aunt remained firmly in charge.

"Never mind the outward form," said the old lady, toothless and almost bald. "Let men have the outward say, they must have a face. But keep control; keep a firm hand on everything. They will not rebel, they will accept it."

With that, she would shuffle off on her tiny feet—bound, in traditional style when she was young—to supervise the serving of dinner, or the counting of money for employees of the Lee tribe who lived together in a substantial complex of houses, surrounding a dusty interior courtyard with its withered plum trees.

Cynthia had come a long way from Suchow. But she applied the traditional methods of her great-aunt. Simon Wing, Clarence Lam and now Polly were kept in place by a subtle combination of forcefulness when that was necessary and seductiveness which was always needed. And as to sentiment about them, she had none. There was little inspiration to be had from men, nothing to compare to that deep feeling of patriotism for the country, for land. Cynthia was moved by the idea of her homeland, with its great rolling plains, the mountain ranges, the quiet streams, and the watered paddy fields. A vast canvas vibrant and alive. It was something she could give her life for.

Polly suggested a walk along the Praia Grande, with its ostentatious mansions lining the boulevard. As the light faded in the bay, the flicker of small lights from fishing boats appeared. A gentle breeze wafted in the trees. It was an idyllic scene.

When they returned to the hotel, hardly having exchanged a word in the taxi, Cynthia undressed and went straight to bed, lying with her back facing the middle of the bed.

# Chapter 20

Returning from Macao had been a depressing business. When they returned to Hong Kong, Cynthia gave him a hasty peck and then disappeared into the thronging crowds of Des Voeux Road. There had been no question of going to her flat. She had made that quite clear. Instead, Polly went straight home though he did not relish arriving at the empty house. When he had emptied the contents of his suitcase onto the bed in the spare room—Ah Hing would sort them out the next day—Polly went to his study and put the sheet with the poem on his desk, next to the fine fountain pen that Clarence had given him.

How different Clarence seemed from Cynthia. How much more gentle, even more physically delicate. But was he too just a fellow-travelling friend? Someone who one had to do a job with? Polly was tired of having to struggle to understand the nuances of a difficult, barely penetrable, foreign culture.

The next day was going to be a rather heavy one. To try to cheer her up, Polly and Anthony Bridges had agreed to take Susan Chowder out to lunch.

"Where should we go?" Polly asked Anthony Bridges.

"Oh, there is only one place on a Sunday," came the breezy reply, "the Repulse Bay Hotel. If we run out of conversation with Susan, we can always get Margaret da Sousa, the house manager who also lives there, to join us."

Polly nodded in agreement. Actually, he rather enjoyed the company of Margaret da Sousa who had an endless stock of stories about the many guests she had seen coming and going from the hotel. Under its roof, it seemed that anything could happen—and almost everything had happened—and Margaret da Sousa had seen it all.

The three companions set off in a taxi and were soon descending into the beautiful bay. Arriving early, they were ushered to the terrace which, in its slightly elevated position gave a magnificent view of the bay and protected guests from the hawkers hanging around outside the entrance. Anthony Bridges led the way to his favourite table near one of the columns that gave the building its unmistakable colonial appearance.

"It's awfully nice of you to askkk mee out," spluttered Susan Chowder, "I don't think I've lunched here before."

No sooner had Anthony Bridges ordered three cocktails than the elegantly dressed but portly, Margaret da Sousa appeared.

"Oh, what a distinguished gathering," she said with a smile, "it's not every day that we are so honoured."

"Come and join us, Margaret," said Anthony Bridges motioning to one of the house boys to bring over an extra chair. "It's a pleasure to see you. What's been going on here recently? Any interesting gossip?"

"Well, as a matter of fact," she replied, quickly glancing round to check that no one was nearby who might hear them, "we had the Colonial Secretariat brigade here last night and one or two of them overdid it."

"How amusing," said Anthony Bridges, but before he could continue, Polly intervened.

"Was a certain gentleman, you know who Margaret, one of them?" Margaret da Sousa smiled. She nodded so they all knew it was Alistair Crowley who had been one of the miscreants. They all laughed aloud. So, he who was always so critical of the behaviour of the dons, had his lapses as well.

"Now," said Margaret sensing that it was wise to move off the subject, "what would you like for lunch? We have some excellent, fresh lobster which I can recommend. Or do you prefer something less messy, Susan?"

"Oh, thatt soundss very good," said Susan, "and light too."

"And while we are waiting for our lunch, tell us more about the hotel. How long have you been working here?" Polly asked.

Margaret smiled. "Well, you folks like your history so let's begin at the beginning. The hotel was founded in 1920 with quite a fanfare. It was going to turn Repulse Bay, a bit of a backwater, into the Menton of Hong Kong. I started about five years after that, as a young lass."

"Was that tricky?" Anthony Bridges interjected, "After all, you were a Macao girl."

"You mean for a Eurasian girl," said Margaret with a smile. "I was lucky. The first general manager was a charming gentleman who wasn't concerned at my background but thought I would do well."

"As you have," said Anthony Bridges deciding that it was best to stir off the subject. "And there have been a succession of celebrities staying here, haven't there?"

"Oh yes," Margaret replied, "the latest of whom was William Holden when they were filming *Love is a many Splendored Thing*."

Suddenly, Susan Chowder seemed to come to life. "But nottt asss good as the novel."

"As always," said Polly, "and any writers?"

"Hemingway took up residence for a while. I remember he was typing away right here on the terrace. When I asked him if he was finishing work, he told me it was only garbage, a first draft. But he seemed quite calm about that."

As they spoke, other guests started to appear on the terrace.

"Work beckons," said Margaret with a smile and got out of her chair to greet the guests.

Lunch proved to be a huge success. Polly had to admit that the location was perfect, and the food was excellent. Susan Chowder had relaxed, an achievement in itself. It was almost five in the afternoon before they got back to the university.

A book lay open on his desk. Polly had written out the words of a Persian ode.

*See you anemones their leaves unfold*
*With rubies flaming, and with living gold,*
*While crystal showers from weeping clouds descend*
*Enjoy the presence of thy tuneful friend,*
*Now, while the wines are brought, the sofa lay'd,*
*Be gay: too soon the flowers of spring will fade.*

"Oh, I recognise that, Polly," said Anthony Bridges when he was installed comfortably in the armchair of Polly's study the day after Polly and Cynthia had returned from Macao.

"That's your William Jones again, the Ode of Mesihi."

"Yes, you're right," said Polly, irritated with Anthony Bridges' habit, no doubt picked up during his time in the War Office, of reading anything he found on other people's desks.

Installed once again in his familiar surroundings, Polly reverted to his favourite theme.

"Tell me, Anthony, have you thought any more about the subject we discussed the other day?"

"Oh God, Polly, are you off again? You mean ideas and action, that again?"

"I mean your facetious dismissal of history, Anthony."

"I didn't dismiss history, my dear fellow. I merely said that it is important to recognise what you are doing. I know you have talked a great deal—and written rather less—about 'ultimate history', a kind of history that will be settled, irrefutable."

"A history that will not be a mere narrative?" Polly said.

"Or mythology?" Anthony Bridges said.

"You know very well what I mean, Anthony. Most of the time we are stuck in the realm of documentary history. All we do is to rearrange facts, and then add bibliographies, appendices, God knows what. It doesn't get us anywhere near the interpretative stage I am talking about."

"Polly, your 'ultimate history' is a construct, an ideal type against which reality is measured. But you seem to want to make an inescapable logical connection between them."

"So, history has no laws?"

"That would be an inference," said Anthony Bridges, now quite serious. "I just don't see how one relates historical laws, if you want to call them that, to the events of politics, for example. I cannot see a necessary connection."

Polly did not pursue the matter any further. He was convinced. Anthony Bridges was right. They were dealing with inferences, trends and subjective interpretations of the facts. Of course, the historian searched for cause and effect, but he couldn't test them conclusively. As to the relationship between ideas, political ideas and action, the gulf seemed impassable. For the first time in several weeks, Polly began to hear the familiar buzzing in his ears. He tried to get rid of it by shaking his head, but it had no effect. This time the buzzing was low but persistent, like the traffic one hears in the background in a city, never entirely fading away.

Anthony Bridges saw Polly's movement and guessed at its reason.

"Don't take all this to heart, my dear chap," he said cheerfully, "no one has ever died of unsolved philosophical problems, you know."

"But considerations of this sort could change one's life," said Polly, "affect what one might do…"

He trailed off.

"Many things might change our lives, Polly," said Anthony Bridges, "but that is a matter of psychology and could even become a problem for psychoanalysis. Nothing to do with the objective charting of reality."

Polly stared at his colleague. Four days left before a major catastrophe in capitalist society and here he was discussing the difficulties of charting objective reality with Anthony Bridges. How absurd, how ridiculous was the intellectual life? Their speculations would not influence the likes of Simon Wing or Cynthia Lee—they were actors who did not pause to examine the meaning of their lines. And what of Chief Inspector Chan, playing against them? He might enjoy intellectual games, but no philosophical theory about history was ever going to stop him. And what of his warning to Polly—next time (an ominous-sounding phrase that reminded Polly of school) it would all be up? Polly pondered on that warning. The chief inspector would not put it aside because of the proposition that the connection between political action and philosophical principle was tenuous.

And always in the background—or in the foreground—was his image of Cynthia, her lithe figure, the black blouse thrown on the bed, her bare white breasts, the intoxicating mixture of her Oriental smell and the French perfume that she wore. The Cynthia whom Polly knew was not attached to him or to anyone. The Cynthia whom he knew softened him up, satisfied him entirely and only for the cause. And what had Cynthia done that was in any case out of her Chinese tradition? Had she not been in a family where the third aunt, to satisfy the third uncle, had recruited pretty, young girls from the countryside outside Suchow? Hadn't Cynthia herself, as a teenager, seen doe-eyed creatures, with blanched skin and high cheekbones, wheeled into the compound, dressed and coiffured by third aunt?

"Put away that green handkerchief, master cannot abide that colour! Gold teeth? Oh yes, the third uncle approves, no difficulty."

The old dame recited endless instructions: the way to make third uncle's tea, how his shoes must be put away, and his habits in bed. She rasped out her commands to the awkward novices. Was it angry impatience with their gaucherie or was it the last pained protest of a woman abandoned, scraping what dignity she could out of the title of the first concubine? That had been Cynthia's upbringing. And later she learnt the dark arts herself and practised them with skill. To think that she would be distracted by sentiment, that she could put aside all that harsh experience was as absurd as expecting Ah Tang, the gardener, to suddenly deliver a lecture in fluent English. It just wasn't going to happen.

# Chapter 21

"Polly," said Anthony Bridges suddenly breaking in on his thoughts and reminding Polly that he was still there. "Have you heard the latest about Clarence?"

"No," said Polly, "what's happened now?"

"Well, this time I think he has had it," said Anthony Bridges. "He's going to be sent down. Things are a good deal worse than anyone suspected. You remember when he was locked up in Wanchai at the time of the riots?"

Polly nodded. It seemed such a long time ago. Before he got involved. Before Cynthia.

"They found names and addresses in his papers. Yes, I know, Polly, you won't approve of that, searching through private papers is an unsavoury business, I agree. But this was serious stuff, Polly. Chief Inspector Chan came to see the dean." He paused for a moment. "It seems that there is a cell, a Communist cell, in our midst."

"But what does that matter," said Polly, trying to stifle his rage, "if there is no connection between political ideas and historical happenings?"

Anthony Bridges smiled.

"In terms of logic, nothing at all. But I don't think the chief inspector is operating at that level, though he's no fool. You know he has direct links with Government House. It's all highly political. They are going to be quite ruthless, want to make an example of Clarence *pour discourager les autres.*"

"But that's absurd," Polly retorted. "They are only students; they are meant to be in our care. They trust us. We pontificate about values, about freedom. We teach them to read John Stuart Mill and all that and then the next minute, if they dare to apply any of it, they're in trouble. What hypocrisy, what frauds we are."

Anthony Bridges looked uncomfortable. He gulped down the last of his pink gin and lifted his heavy frame from the rattan chair.

"That may be so. But intellectual fun on the campus is one thing…"

150

"And being serious outside the gates is another?" Polly said and stood up.

"I don't like it any more than you do, Polly, but it's outside our control. Don't interfere, Polly, don't do anything foolish."

With those sombre words, Anthony Bridges walked out of Polly's study, downstairs and out of the front door.

Polly sank back into his chair. He looked around his study, lined with books, read, annotated and surrounded by card indexes and files. And what did it all amount to? Just intelligent, amusing fantasy, quite unrelated to life or to any events that form history?

Polly suddenly started. Wasting time again on thoughts instead of acting. He had better go to see Clarence, find out exactly what had happened, and see if he could help in any way. As he walked across the campus, Laura Li came past with a grim expression on her face. She did not respond to Polly's greeting, which filled him with unease. Could it be that they held him responsible for what had happened? Could Cynthia have reported that he had been behaving oddly ever since the Macao trip, that somehow his manner had changed? Perhaps he was having second thoughts. The cell must have met. They must have considered how further information on Clarence had been obtained. Someone had warned the authorities of his inclination. His room had been searched. Polly was, after all, his moral tutor. He would surely have been consulted before such a serious step as rustication had been considered.

Polly reached Clarence's door and hesitated a moment. Then he knocked. There was a shifting noise inside, the sound of a drawer closing.

"Just a mo," said Clarence in his impeccable public-school best.

A few moments later, he flung the door open and, seeing Polly standing there, made a sweeping gesture that he should enter.

"Well, what an honour, a visit from an eminent historian to a humble student, and not even that for much longer."

There was no rancour in his voice, not a trace of bitterness. If he was annoyed, there was not the slightest hint of it in his face. Polly came in and sat down on one of Clarence's Ming chairs. His room was decorated in the opulent style of students from wealthy Chinese families.

"Clarence, I've only just heard the news. It's outrageous. I was on my way to see the dean to try to get the decision rescinded."

Clarence stared at Polly. His lush, black hair fell forward over his forehead. Polly noticed, for the thousandth time, how exquisite his skin was, like fine porcelain of the most delicate type. In a flash of self-recognition, he saw that what he liked in Clarence's face was its femininity. It could be the face of a woman.

"That's jolly decent of you, Mr Polly, but you shouldn't waste your time. In any case, associating with dissidents—that's what the dean told me I am—won't do you any good. You know the British way—guilt by association. Anyone friendly with a cad must be a cad himself."

Polly did not answer at once. What an exotic mixture Clarence was, with his outwardly English manners and subtle Oriental way of thinking. He was a match for anyone.

"I can imagine what you must be thinking," said Polly, "but I wanted to say that we don't all approve, you know."

"Approve or disapprove, Mr Polly, it doesn't matter. Was it not you who said we must detach ourselves from personal reactions to become better historians, to prepare ourselves for 'ultimate history'?"

Polly knew that Clarence had intended to hurt him if only a little. And then only because he had been hurt himself.

"Perhaps being a historian is less important than being a person, Clarence, a human being deciding on values, deciding on when it is right to take a stand."

"I dare say that's true," said Clarence with a flourish, "but nothing so awful is about to happen to me. I'm not going to become a decent human being."

Polly grinned at Clarence's undergraduate wit, undaunted even in such extreme circumstances.

"But tell me, Mr Polly, how are you? How was Macao?"

Polly felt uneasy. He did not like the idea of the circle discussing the intimacies of his affair with Cynthia.

"You do understand, Mr Polly," continued Clarence before he could respond, "that Chinese women are not interested in what you might call romantic attachments, least of all with foreigners. It would be a great mistake to think that they were."

Polly reddened. So, the cell had met; they had been discussing him.

"I haven't found any woman to be romantic in the sense you are talking about, Clarence. I think it is men who are the romantics."

Clarence smiled.

"You are right, Mr Polly, as in so much else. And since we are speaking so candidly, may I say how much I have been honoured by what you have done for me and touched by your care for me. I will never forget that."

They both stood in silence. Outside there was the sound of a car on the driveway; the breeze rustled the leaves outside the window. Polly was lost for words. Looking at Clarence, he realised how important this boy had become to him, how empty his life was going to be without him. He stood and moved towards Clarence who had turned to face the window so the tears in his eyes would not be seen. Polly gently placed his hand on Clarence's shoulder, let it rest there for a moment, and then withdrew it. He moved back towards the door.

As he was about to open it, Clarence turned to face him.

"It's tomorrow, Mr Polly," he whispered, "it is tomorrow."

# Chapter 22

Polly's mind was ablaze with thoughts. Everything seemed to crowd in on him at once—the packed lecture room, Laura Li's cynical grin, Clarence's tearful farewell, Fiona in the garden. When he went out for an evening meal at the students' canteen, he noticed the light on in the dean's study, curious that he should still be there at that hour. None of Polly's students were present, so he ate in solitary silence. On his way home, he saw a figure lurking at the side of his house. Clearly, he was being watched. But he did not care whether he was being watched or not. All he could think about were Clarence's last words and his sincerity, the deep emotion that lay behind what he had said. It was no use dwelling any longer on possibilities and the all-too-fine balance of reasoning. No use weighing and balancing alternatives. The time had come to act.

The next day was crisp and cool. The day of judgement had come. He would never sit calmly on his balcony enjoying the peace and quiet before Ah Hing's arrival. He had woken; it was true, a little earlier than usual and found his passionate companion painfully stiff and upright. He lay for some moments in bed, already covered in sweat, anticipating what lay ahead. He could hear his own thoughts as clearly as a bell; no interference, no annoyance, calm and mellifluous the sound of his own inner voice. When Polly got up, he noticed an unusual lightness in his head, a feeling of floating, even flying, which was often the subject of his dreams. He could not remember feeling any better than he did for many years. For the first time in his life, he felt in full control of his own destiny.

Polly moved about the house purposefully, performing his morning functions with a lightness of touch. There was nothing to stop him now, no buzzing in his head, no threats from the dean, no Alistair Crowley nor Anthony Bridges nor even Cynthia, the unfeeling one. Even the appearance of Ah Hing, who for once seemed to get his morning eggs right, could dampen his spirits. Sitting at his desk only in his white underpants, he penned a short essay, a prediction of what would happen that day and, in its own way, an explanation. He left it in a prominent position, just as he had written it, the four manuscript pages, written in dark ink, lying side by side on his desk.

Polly chose his clothes carefully. He decided on something more festive than usual, something that might express a little of the excitement he felt within himself. He reached for one of his best, striped blue shirts, a yellow spotted tie and his hat—a little battered, but still acceptable if he punched it out gently. Then he began to pack his bag with all the essentials he needed for his business, clandestine business—fuses, ignition leads, combustible material, a mask against the smoke. It was all there, all arranged neatly so that it might have been mistaken by the innocent for a picnic bag.

In a short while, clutching the bag, Polly strolled out of No. 3, down towards the university gates, then along a sloping, hilly street that took him to the tram line. He would take the tram, the most democratic form of transport, frowned upon by the ex-pats, along Des Voeux Road to Central.

As the tram jangled along the streets, he felt the fresh morning air on his face. He savoured the Chinese smells rising from the side streets of vegetable stores and animal shops and watched the young bank clerks in their smart suits jump on and off the tram as it clanged to a stop. The tram veered into Queen's Road Central, with its old colonial facades and balconies, now used to store every conceivable item of household junk, from metal bed frames to ornate wooden bird-cages. On one tiny square roof, a whole family was already outside slurping congee, their gruel, which might be the only meal of the day until they returned home—for the roof was home—exhausted at night. The heat was already beginning to rise; Polly could feel himself sticking to the seat.

Then suddenly there was an immense commotion. Complete havoc. The tram screeched to a halt. Policemen in khaki uniforms were everywhere. From the road ahead, people were running in the direction of the tram, screaming and wailing.

"Bad *feng shui.*"

"Should never have been allowed."

"End of the world."

The air was rent with shouting and crying. The crowd was dangerously swollen and menacing. Polly could understand that people were screaming about money, demanding their money. Others shouted, "*lai gun, lai gun*—they are coming."

Polly fought his way off the tram, standing on the narrow, crowded platform, he looked ahead to see an enormous cloud of black smoke, the whole sky above the Hong Kong & Shanghai Bank was black. Even at a distance, the flames devouring the building could be seen mixed up in the billowing smoke. It looked as if the whole of Central was alight. Polly suddenly froze. He realised that his bag, full of equipment to start a blaze, would be used as evidence against him. He would be accused of starting the fire. He had been framed.

The crowd behind Polly surged forward and he could feel himself being pushed along. It was impossible to resist the pressure. He was swept forward until the whole mass of bodies was jammed solid in a block. Looking ahead, Polly saw a row of police jeeps parked as a blockade across the road. The mob began to rock them, determined to break past. He had to get rid of his bag. Suddenly Polly made out the figure of an officer, the silver crowns on his lapels glinting in the sun. It was Chief Inspector Chan. He battered his way forward with his cane, shouting hoarsely, "I warned you, Mr Polly, I warned you that we would deal with you the next time. Your bonfire is lit, but we have got you good and proper this time."

**FINISH**